She knew what she wanted...and went for it.

Della looked deeply into Gabe's eyes, hoping she was communicating every bit of desire she was feeling.

"Tell me if I'm overstepping, but do you think our waiter would wrap this dish up so we could take it back to your place?"

Della smiled. Was Gabe asking what she thought he was asking?

"I think he'd do that, yes," she whispered, lifting her face toward his so she spoke close to his mouth, just a breath away from a kiss.

"Good."

The way he said the word, with so much sensual promise, made her shiver.

This was a first for Della, for sure. With the meal paid for, she took Gabe's hand and they moved quickly down the walk, less busy now that the stars were out.

As they passed into the shadow of a streetlight next to a huge tree, Gabe held her back, directed her under the tree. He pulled her up close and looked down into her face. "I've wanted to do this ever since I saw you on that plane."

He kissed her then, and Della's world turned upside down. She'd been kissed before, but certainly not like this...

Dear Reader,

Book settings are so important to me, and I've visited most of the places where I set my stories so that I can capture the details and atmosphere of the location. I like to think the books are a mini-vacation as a reader accompanies my characters on their adventure. In the case of *Hot in the City*, Della Clark and Gabe Ross meet in a place I've been to many times, my home state city, New York.

What I love about New York City is its contrasts: it's a place of glaring neon and noise, big buildings and bigger personalities—but it's also a city with surprisingly quiet corners, quaint, tree-lined streets and beautiful gardens. Gabe and Della experience all of these as part of their own romantic landscape. Of course, the city has its secrets, and so does Gabe. With him, Della is about to discover more adventure than she ever counted on in her hometown.

If you've never been to New York, I highly encourage you to go. But in the meanwhile, you can enjoy some of the sites and atmosphere of the city in this book. As for me, I'm continuing to travel, which means more settings for future books, including new areas of the US as well as Europe. To hear more about where I'm going and the books I'm writing, follow me on Twitter or Facebook, or at The Chocolate Box blog. I love to chat.

Happy Summer,

Sam

Samantha Hunter

Hot in the City

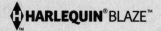

Recycling programs
for this product may
not exist in your area.

ISBN-13: 978-0-373-79857-5

Hot in the City

Copyright © 2015 by Samantha Hunter

Printed in U.S.A.

Samantha Hunter lives in Syracuse, New York, where she writes full-time for Harlequin. When she's not plotting her next story, Sam likes to work in her garden, quilt, cook, read and spend time with her husband and their dogs. Most days you can find Sam chatting on the Harlequin Blaze boards at Harlequin.com, or you can check out what's new, enter contests or drop her a note at her website, samanthahunter.com.

Books by Samantha Hunter

HARLEQUIN BLAZE

Talking in Your Sleep...
Hard to Resist
Caught in the Act
Make Your Move
I'll Be Yours for Christmas
Mine Until Morning
Straight to the Heart
Yours for the Night
Hers for the Holidays
His Kind of Trouble
Unforgettable
Unexpected Temptation
"Holiday Rush" in *Wild Holiday Nights*

To get the inside scoop on Harlequin Blaze and its talented writers, be sure to check out blazeauthors.com.

All backlist available in ebook format.

Visit the Author Profile page at Harlequin.com for more titles.

For my editor, Kathryn, and thanks to all of the Harlequin Blaze editorial staff and production crew I've worked with over the years, for your hard work in making every book shine. With much appreciation.

For all of my friends who put up with me while I'm writing and often kvetching about it—you are all made of gold.

1

As soon as Della Clark settled into her first-class seat, flying back to New York City after a month of consulting on a project in San Diego, she pulled out her tablet to check for progress on her online dating accounts.

Yes, *accounts*—plural.

Statistically speaking, she needed to cast a broad net. Fellow mathematicians had posited that the chances of finding a perfect partner, depending on the variables and location, were about one in two-hundred and eighty-five thousand. Della was pretty sure she hadn't met that many people in her thirty-three years, and true to the math, very few were at all suitable for her. Well, at this point, the sum was actually zero.

On top of that, census numbers showed that there were far more unattached females than available males in the world, and the older a woman got, the more unlikely she—Della, for instance—would be able to find a man her age, thirty-three, or older. It wasn't impossible, of course, just nearly so.

Unless you compromised, but Della didn't want to compromise on love. Or sex. With a few mediocre sexual relationships in her past, she had yet to discover the sex that other women crowed about, the blow-your-mind sort. The kind of sex that made women fall in love with the wrong man—not that she wanted to do that.

Or maybe she did, if only for a while.

People crowded into the plane, but she was oblivious as she studied a few of the suitors' profiles.

Jamie Reynolds was cute, she thought, pursing her lips and tilting her head to the side as she considered his picture. With attractive, masculine features and a good smile, she clicked onto his bio, feeling hopeful. Her hopes were quickly dashed. Among his interests were guns, hunting, and domination. He'd included some extra profile pictures that showed off his very nice body, but it was decked out in leather, with a picture of him carrying a whip and handcuffs slung off a belt at his waist.

Next.

Garrison Gunther.

Garrison had recently moved to New York from Germany, and he was curator of a small international museum. He was in his fifties, but appeared distinguished and intelligent, with no affection for weapons of any kind, that she could tell. Then she saw the note: Need someone who will love and take care of four young children. He wanted a nanny, not a life partner.

Next.

Unfortunately, she had to ditch the next three, as well. Too young, too political and one ex-con.

Oh well, at least she was getting more responses since she let her stylist put the strawberry highlights in her blond hair, and she'd started wearing some lip color and mascara. But she wasn't attracting the right kind of guy. Did they think she was desperate because she was a single, mid-thirties mathematician? That she would take any offer that came along?

Well, she had standards. But perhaps she had cast her net a bit too widely—maybe she needed to revise her profile so that it would attract a slightly more refined range of potential mates.

As the flight attendants instructed that all wireless tech be shut down, she closed her tablet with a sigh. Looking up, she watched a handsome guy walking down the aisle to find his seat.

Nice. Why couldn't someone like him show up on her dating profiles?

Tall, he had to duck slightly as he made his way down the center, a shock of ginger-brown hair falling across his high forehead in a way that made her want to push it back. He reached up to open an overhead compartment and showed off his flat stomach, accentuated by the way his maroon, short-sleeved shirt was tucked into a pair of rugged khakis.

The front of the khakis didn't escape her notice, either. Strong thighs, slim, straight hips and...well, suffice to say he had—er, *was*—the whole package.

Then, he was right in front of her as he settled his computer case into the overhead compartment above her. He turned, slid into the aisle seat next to her and smiled. She was looking into caramel-colored—or were they more café au lait?—eyes that were only inches from hers.

It took her about thirty seconds to realize that his gorgeous lips were moving; talking to her.

Hi, looks like I'm your company for this flight.

Good thing she'd learned to read lips when she was a kid. One of her best friends had been deaf, and Della had never lost the skill.

"Yes," she responded vaguely, still trying to decide on the right adjective for his eye color.

He held his hand out, and she placed hers in his. As his smooth, warm grip closed around hers, she sucked in a breath.

Wow.

Oh heck, had she said that out loud?

"I'm Gabe."

"Della."

He nodded. "Nice to meet you."

"You, too," she replied, removing her hand as soon as he loosened his.

The flight attendant went through the safety spiel, and Della and her neighbor settled back, belted in, secure in their individual space as they took off. Once at altitude, Della let out a sigh of relief and relaxed.

"Don't like takeoffs?" Gabe asked.

She managed a smile. "Not much. Or landings."

"They are the most dangerous parts of the flight, they say."

"Landings are more so, about twenty-six percent more accidents happen on final approach and landings, though the number of fatalities is the same as in accidents during takeoff and the initial climb. Overall, though, the number of fatalities is below one percent for all flights, so it's still the safest way to travel," Della rambled, and then bit her lip, stopping herself.

Yes. *This* would be the reason she almost never had sex.

But Gabe leaned in, looking interested. "You know a lot about safety statistics."

She shrugged, embarrassed. "I read a lot," she hedged, taking off her dark-rimmed glasses and putting them in her pocket. She only needed them for reading, anyway. Maybe this was a good time to do some light research in revising her dating profile. Start with losing the glasses.

"So what do you do, Della?"

Next, don't mention you are a genius mathematician.

"I teach. At Columbia."

His eyebrows lifted. "Impressive. What subject?"

"Math," she said quickly, and then pretended to drop something so she could bend down to reach for it, halting the conversation.

When she rose, he was looking at her closely, his eyes narrowed, studying her expression, as if he could see what she was thinking.

Oh, she hoped not.

"What do *you* do?" she asked brightly, changing the subject as she tried to regain her composure.

He was distracted from answering as the flight attendant approached with the drink cart, at which point Della also surreptitiously noted that Gabe was not wearing any rings.

The attendant also seemed to note that fact as she asked them what they wanted to drink. She made much more eye contact with Gabe than with Della, and when she handed Della her cola, she leaned over enough to give Gabe—and anyone who was looking—a good view down her blouse.

Della had to force herself not to roll her eyes. Though she couldn't blame the guy if he did look; the attendant was practically shoving her breasts in his face.

Della slid her fingers up to the buttons on her blouse.

Maybe she should try unloosening a few. Learn from the experts, they always say.

Instead, she sipped her cola and observed Gabe's smile as the attendant engaged him in a few seconds of small talk—including letting him know she was on a weekend layover once they got into New York.

Subtle. *Not*.

Della stared out the window at the cloud layer, enjoying the view and pretending not to hear their conversation.

Suddenly, a warm hand closed around hers, and she nearly jumped out of her seat. Gabe's fingers squeezed hers slightly, stemming her startled response.

"Thanks, but my girl Della and I are on an anniversary trip. Three weeks this weekend since we met."

Gabe lifted her hand and kissed it, and Della simply let him, too surprised to do otherwise. The flight attendant looked like she wanted to gag.

"Well, then, enjoy your weekend." Her smile was forced as her eyes met Della's, with no small amount of disbelief.

As the attendant moved on, Della extricated her hand and whispered, "What did you say that for?"

Gabe shrugged. "She was being rude, and I wasn't interested. Thanks for helping out."

Della laughed. "She probably didn't believe we're together for a second."

"Why not?"

She leveled him a disbelieving look. He was being completely serious. This incredibly hot man had no notion why a very sexy woman would not believe he was with *her*.

"Have you looked in a mirror lately?" she asked with a laugh.

He shook his head, staring back at her. "Have you?" he asked in the same tone.

Surprise choked off any reply.

"We should keep the ruse up, don't you think?" he asked with a wiggle of his eyebrows and a grin that Della was helpless to resist.

She was more than willing to play.

"Sure. Why not?"

He leaned in closer. "This is a delicate undercover project. You'll do whatever I need you to do," he teased mischievously.

Della almost giggled.

"Well, nothing that could put me on a no-fly list."

"That leaves a lot we *could* do," he said, and though she knew he was only flirting, having some fun, there was a look in his eye that threw her off. Like he was enjoying this as much as she was.

"Well, it's only been three weeks. And I've been out of town for most of that time. I'm not sure we've had sex yet," she said primly.

He chuckled and leaned in. "Oh, honey, we had sex the first night, and almost every night after. We can't keep our hands off each other. It's the most amazing sex of your life," he said, gloating.

Della's pulse raced at the thought. "You're pretty confident. And apparently I'm very…easy."

He nodded. "See? We're like peanut butter and jelly."

Again, he made her laugh. Unsure what to say, she resorted to reaching into her bag for a deck of cards she always carried with her.

"Play cards?" she asked.

"What game?"

"Solitaire."

"How about poker? Maybe we could make it interesting, if you're a girl who likes to gamble."

"No gambling for me," she said with a shake of her head.

"Addiction?" he asked, very seriously.

"No, I'm just…really good." She glanced at him from under her lashes, hoping he bought it. "I always win."

One brow raised. "Lots of college poker parties?"

"Something like that."

The truth was that she won because she couldn't help but count the cards and mentally calculate odds. It had almost gotten her into hot water at a casino once.

"Well, now you've made me curious. No stakes, but let's see if you're as good as you say you are."

She smiled, taking out the cards and shuffling them quite expertly, which drew another impressed glance from her sexy neighbor.

"Don't say I didn't warn you."

He was toast.

Della took the majority of the hands over the course of the flight, but she admired how Gabe didn't give up. She also liked that he wasn't a sore loser. In fact, he seemed to have a lot of fun with her, unlike other men she'd played cards with. They never liked a woman winning all the time.

If there had been stakes, she would have cleaned him out.

Gabe managed to win a few hands. He was a clever

player, and though he wasn't counting cards, he was a shrewd observer and had a great poker face.

He won the last hand as the captain announced their imminent arrival, his grin wide.

"Too bad I didn't bet a kiss on that last hand."

"I, um, er," she mumbled as she almost dropped the cards while putting them back in the box.

He caught them, sliding his hand over hers as he did so.

She held her breath as they started their descent. Gabe didn't release her hand, but squeezed it reassuringly.

If she was going to die in an airplane, this was definitely the way to go.

Except that she hoped that maybe...would he want to see her after they landed? Should she perhaps suggest dinner? Or maybe just a drink? Would he think she was asking for more?

Was she?

It took so much time to work up her nerve that she didn't even realize they were already speeding down the runway, then rolling to the gate.

She swallowed—this was the time. Now or never.

What was the worst he could say? No? He was definitely flirting with her, so there was a chance, right?

But as she released her held breath, he freed her hand, standing quickly as people jockeyed for position to leave the plane. He stepped back, gesturing for her to exit in front of him.

"Ladies first."

Della was overly aware of his big body behind her, crowding her slightly as she reached up and grabbed her bag, his front bumping up against her back, especially when he reached forward to get his own bag, leaning over her.

Ask him. Now.

Then they were moving forward, out of the plane, up the jet bridge, pushed along by the momentum of the people around them, all hurrying to exit.

She turned, and Gabe was looking at his watch, frowning, his expression suddenly distant.

"Gabe, I—"

"Della, it was great to meet you. Thanks for the company and the cards," he said quickly, obviously distracted. "Sorry, I have to run." He offered a smile before he turned in the opposite direction, walking off.

She waved, though he wasn't looking anymore.

Della blinked, her cheeks burning as she started walking away, disappointed and embarrassed. In a flash, she was back in the hallway of her junior high, younger than the other kids in her class, with a crush on a cute boy who laughed when she waved and said hi and then kept on walking. Then, like now, it felt like everyone had seen her make a fool of herself— that they were all looking at her—though that wasn't so, of course.

Back in school, the boys liked to flirt with her so she would help them with their math, but when it came to parties and dances, she was never included. She knew why, but at least when she helped them with their studies, they talked to her. Her parents had warned her constantly to keep to herself, that people would always want to use her for something. That she couldn't be gullible and trusting. That she was meant for more important things than boys and parties.

Their advice had been true often enough. Gabe had

only been looking for some amusement on the flight, nothing more. She shouldn't have made more of it, knowing better.

Swallowing her letdown, she refocused her thoughts on work as she rode into the city, alone. As usual.

GABRIEL ROSS—AT LEAST, that was the name he was using for the moment—made it to his hotel still thinking about the woman on the plane. His lips kicked up into a smile as he thought about her, but he killed it. This was work. *She* was work.

Still, he was human. And male. Sitting so closely on the plane, he'd had more than one fantasy about how easy it would be to pick her up and do any number of arousing things to her, she was so petite. If he released her strawberry-blond hair from its sharply pulled back ponytail, how would it frame her heart-shaped face? How would she like to be kissed? How would she taste?

He'd love to find out what else made her blush. Watching her tightly rounded rear end as she walked ahead of him on the jet bridge had driven him crazy. He'd been close to asking her to dinner. Maybe for more than dinner.

It wasn't often anyone—man or woman—beat him at poker. But of course, it would be tough to beat someone with her card-counting skills. She might be able to fool the average person, but Gabe was trained to notice such things. Once he'd figured out her game, he was able to take a few hands. It hadn't been easy, though. He'd enjoyed the challenge.

But she also wasn't a random person he'd met at the airport. She was his target. Or one of them. Dr. Olive

Delilah Clark—Della, as she'd been called since she was young—was someone he needed to get close to.

Someone had been leaking sensitive data about the development of a vaccine for biological weapons at a NYC-based biotech firm, and it was Gabe's job to find out who it was. They'd only gotten part of the research, and would no doubt be making an attempt to get more. So DHS planted dummy research, hoping the culprits went for the bait.

However, the perpetrator clearly had an inside contact, or a back-door in, to access the company's research computers, which were offline. Gabe needed to get inside and find out who that contact was, and how the spies were accomplishing their task.

He'd be going in as a DHS investigator doing routine security checks on the staff members who worked on military contracts. In reality, he'd be running deep surveillance and peeking under the covers to see what secrets the lab's employees might be hiding.

Anyone who was particularly interesting would merit deeper investigation. It meant digging into people's lives—their private lives—and doing whatever it took to stop the leak.

Della had worked for the company as a contractor in the past, on the vaccine project, though the details were above her civilian security clearance. She finished her work in the early stages of the project, but that didn't mean she escaped suspicion. She was an outlier, a random element, but that made her particularly interesting. She might be completely innocent, but it was also possible she had been turned or was being compelled by foreign agents. She was also smart—so he had to be smarter.

Gabe grabbed the computer bag he'd taken from the plane and slung it up on the wide table in front of the couch. He took pictures with his phone as he opened it, so he could replicate the case when he put it back together. An e-reader in a bright purple plastic skin appeared, and several foreign-language tapes tumbled out onto the floor.

Della's bag. He'd done his homework, bringing along a similar bag of his own and taking hers "by mistake."

The tapes were for learning Italian, but what he was most interested in was the laptop. There were no other papers of consequence in the case. He fired up his own machine, which had been waiting for him in the car, and started the password-breaking software he needed to get into Della's computer.

While it ran, he filtered through her other belongings. Opening the laptop, he raised an eyebrow at the spreadsheet labeled "potentials" and found a list of names—male names—with comments and traits listed. Then he saw the links to online profiles—not spies, but online dating profiles.

Della was trying to find men online? That surprised him, and he went through the profiles, checking out each one in detail. In the process of doing so, he became irritated at the idea of Della actually dating any of these losers. She was better than this.

A beep signaled him that the password had been found, and he turned his attention to her laptop, allowing him to skim her files and download everything to his computer. There were several locked folders, and those he would need more time to investigate. He put the case back together exactly as he'd found it and checked his watch.

How long would it be before she noticed that she had the wrong bag and contacted him? It was imperative that she initiate their next contact. It would make her feel in control.

He couldn't deny that he was looking forward to seeing her again. The opportunity to get closer to Dr. Clark was a tempting one, and while part of the job, he didn't usually feel this keen a sense of anticipation at the prospect. What he'd found so far, unless there was more in the files, required only a general surveillance. He wanted to learn more.

For better or worse.

It was a rationalization, of course. He also wanted to have sex with her; he could be honest with himself about that much.

Sitting back, he pulled the laptop toward him, starting to study the files, and waited for the phone to ring. He had no doubt that it would.

2

DELLA SLOWED HER PACE as she approached the restaurant where she was meeting Gabe Ross. She'd been shocked when she'd opened her bag and realized it wasn't hers. Especially when she'd discovered the stack of papers with the Homeland Security letterhead and his badge inside. She'd closed it as quickly as possible, calling him immediately.

She'd been so flustered on the plane that she'd clearly grabbed the wrong bag.

Still, she thought with a smile playing around her lips, it had resulted in her seeing Gabe again. It had taken every ounce of nerve to call him after discovering the mistake and finding his contact information on the luggage tag.

As she approached the small café with tables on the sidewalk under a charming dark red canopy, she heard her name called and looked up to see Gabe standing by the door.

Della walked quickly toward him, seeing that he had her case as well.

"I'm so sorry," she said, grimacing. "I could have

had this sent to you, instead of dragging you all the
way up here."

He smiled, taking his case as he handed her hers.
"This is much better. I wouldn't have wanted the case
in unfamiliar hands."

"Oh, yes, I—" she said, dropping her eyes down,
then meeting his again. "I didn't look through your
things, of course, but I did open it and saw you work
for the government. I promise I only saw the letterhead
and your badge and then closed it right away."

"I appreciate that," he said. "Your things should be
intact. I didn't know we'd switched until you called."

Then one of the waiters, Gianni, appeared, smiling
in her direction.

"Ciao, Gianni. Come stai? Avete una tavola libera?"

"Ho sempre una tavolo per voi, bella," Gianni said
fondly, grabbing menus and leading them to a table
on the patio.

Gabe looked at her. "You speak Italian, too?"

"Not as well as I'd like to. I have a chance to go to
Italy as a visiting lecturer this fall, but I haven't made
up my mind yet. So I practice when I can."

"Grazie, Gianni," she said, smiling at the older man.
"This is Gabe."

"Nice to meet you, Gabe," the waiter said, and Della
almost had to chuckle at how Gianni smiled, but his
eyes narrowed on Gabe as he took their drink orders.

"A close friend?" Gabe inquired when Gianni disappeared back inside.

"I tutored his youngest daughter so she could im-
prove her math scores for college, and I wrote her a rec-
ommendation. I spent several evenings at their home,

and here at the restaurant, teaching her, so I did get to be friends with the family. They are a lovely group."

"Did she end up getting into the school she wanted?"

"She did. Full scholarship to Cornell in veterinary science." Della smiled, proud of her friend, and that she could help.

"Did you grow up here, in the city?" Gabe asked.

"No, I was born in Connecticut, and I spent a good deal of my teenage years in Boston."

She stopped there, not elaborating that she had spent her teenage years in Massachusetts because she had been admitted to Harvard when she was fifteen. She'd finished her first PhD by the time she was twenty, and then a second at twenty-four.

"When did you start working at Columbia?"

"About eight years ago. New York is home now. I can't imagine being anywhere else."

"But you travel a lot?"

"I do. I do work as a consultant on several government and private-sector projects in addition to teaching, and I visit universities in different countries. It's a great excuse to travel." She paused as Gianni delivered their wine and took their orders, then turned the discussion away from herself. "So, you work for DHS? That has to be exciting."

"Actually, most of my work is at my desk. I do a lot of strategic analysis, that kind of thing. Writing analyst reports and giving advice on operations."

"Oh, I love logisitics!" Della said enthusiastically, and then bit her lip.

"What's the matter?" he asked.

"Oh, I know I can get geeky about things like that, you know, it can put people off."

To her surprise, he frowned, and then reached over to touch her hand, which rested on the table by her wineglass.

"You shouldn't hold back when you're excited about something," he said, staring into her eyes so intently that she couldn't look away.

She also wondered for a second if he knew how excited she was about being here with him—and how he was touching her hand.

Then she chastised herself for making the same mistake she'd made on the plane, being too hopeful. This was just a dinner, and he was only being nice. He wouldn't even be here if it weren't for the bag switch.

"Thank you," she said, gently disentangling her hand from his—or trying. When she pulled away, he curled his fingers around hers, and squeezed. Then he let go.

Oh my.

"Besides, it's not every day someone finds my work interesting, either. They imagine feds are always busting down doors or hauling in bad guys, but for me, it's a lot of paperwork. Which is fine. I had enough action in the army."

"You served?"

"Ten years, four tours to Iraq and Afghanistan."

Della watched his features change as he talked, how his smile faded and his eyes became shadowed.

"And you came home and joined DHS?"

"I actually went back to college first, something I hadn't had the time to do back before I joined the military. But school wasn't my thing—never really was. My military experience was more valuable, for DHS, anyway. So I talked to some contacts, and that was where I ended up five years ago."

"What were you studying in school? Where did you go?"

"Virginia Tech. I thought I'd do something with IT, but it wasn't where my strengths were."

"So you live in Virginia?"

"Well, D.C. now."

She sighed, fighting the well of admiration and sheer lust that his story aroused in her. He was military, he served his country and he continued to do that. A hero.

A handsome, sexy, amazing hero. Here at dinner, with her.

Their dinners arrived, which was a good thing, before Della made a fool out of herself fawning all over him. As much as she loved the food here, Della barely tasted anything as she ate her chicken piccata.

And as she lifted a tender bite of meat to her lips, she met his eyes and realized he was watching her, his own dinner untouched as he observed her with an intense, hot look.

"I'm sorry," he said, shaking his head as if to break the trance, but his gaze found its way back to her mouth again as she took the bite. "I just…you're very beautiful. I guess I shouldn't say things like that. For all I know, you're married, or with someone else."

The words made her catch her breath and she coughed.

Gabe was around the table in a second, his arms around her, lifting her from the chair, but her breath came back before any action was needed.

"I'm okay…it's gone," she said.

He didn't remove his arms, at least not right away. Della straightened, but that only brought their bodies closer together. It seemed natural to place her hand on his at her waist.

"Thank you, but to answer your question, there's no one at the moment."

Gabe leaned his face down into her neck, breathing in, and then he spoke low by her ear.

"I'm glad to hear that. Tell me if I'm overstepping, but do you think Gianni would wrap this up so we could take it back to your place?"

Her heart slammed in her chest. Was he asking what she thought he was asking? She wasn't sure what to say…but Della knew what she *wanted*, and went for it.

"I think he'd do that, yes," she whispered, lifting her face toward his so she spoke close to his mouth, just a breath away from a kiss.

"Good."

The way he said the word, with so much sensual promise, made her skin ripple with pinpricks of sensation.

"Though I'm not really that hungry," she added as she met his eyes when he stepped away.

"I am. Starving," he said against her ear, and she shivered, knowing he didn't mean he wanted their leftovers.

Della's mind spun; this was a first in her life, for sure. Gianni knew to put dinner on her tab, and so she took Gabe's hand and they walked quickly down the walk, less busy now after dark had fallen.

As they passed into the shadow of a streetlight under a huge tree, Gabe grabbed her hand, stopping her from moving forward. Stepping back under the tree, he pulled her up close and looked down into her face.

"I've wanted to do this ever since I saw you on the plane."

He kissed her, and Della's world turned upside down. She was pretty sure she had never been kissed before, certainly not like this.

Gabe took control, keeping her tight against him, sliding his tongue between her lips, urging her to open, which she did, so willingly she should have been embarrassed.

But she wasn't.

Instead, she pressed in close, wound her arms around his neck and made a few forays of her own, nipping at his bottom lip and then licking the spot, making him groan in approval.

She was close enough that she could feel the hard ridge of his arousal against her belly, and that triggered her own libido, too. Still, somewhere in the back of her mind, all she could think was, is this really happening?

"Yes, it really is," he whispered against her mouth. "As long as you want it to."

She closed her eyes, her cheeks aflame. Good thing it was so dark. "I can't believe I said that out loud."

"I was thinking it, too," he reassured her, dipping in for another kiss. "You're delicious."

His compliment made her blush and laugh softly against his mouth. No one had ever told her she was *delicious*.

"Let's go," she said, echoing his sentiment from the restaurant.

He grabbed her hand, and they hurried from their hiding spot under the sprawl of the tree, and within minutes she was opening the door and holding her breath, nerves assaulting her again.

She ignored her doubts and inner demons, turning to Gabe and taking matters into her own hands. She pressed up against him, flattening him to the wall of the entryway—he went willingly—and tugged him down by his shirt collar for more kissing.

Merely kissing Gabe was already better than any sex she'd ever had before. Della couldn't wait to see what would come next.

"I like a woman who knows what she wants," he managed to say in between deep, wet kisses that she could easily find addicting.

She pulled back and, remembering the moment on the plane when she'd first seen him, she reached up and pushed the recalcitrant shock of hair, which always fell forward, back in place.

He smiled at that and captured her hand with his, bringing it to his lips.

"Upstairs, then?"

Della nodded and turned toward the stairs, but was swamped with sudden doubt. She'd never done this before, meeting a man she barely knew and taking him home to bed. Taking him to her room, her sanctuary, was too intimate, crazy as that seemed considering what they were about to do, and she faltered as she crossed the entry.

His hands cupped her shoulders, rubbing lightly.

"Everything okay?"

Was it?

What if she disappointed him? He was clearly more experienced and more at ease. *What if…?*

"I can leave. It's okay, Della" he said reassuringly.

She took a deep breath and turned to face him.

"I'm sorry. Cold feet, I guess. Do you mind if we… stay downstairs?"

"Sure. Listen, let's sit, have a glass of wine and talk. There's no pressure. I've enjoyed your company, and whether this goes further or not, that doesn't change."

The sincerity in his voice did her in. That was sexier than anything, and Della was quite sure she wasn't going to let him leave until after they had both gotten naked. But a glass of wine sounded good, too.

"Thank you. I do have a nice white wine that I haven't opened yet. If you want to go in and sit, I can get it from the fridge."

"Sounds perfect," he said, leaning in to kiss the side of her neck, sending sparks dancing over her skin.

Della hurried with the wine, hoping Gabe didn't change his mind, and she almost heaved a sigh of relief when she found him settled comfortably on the sofa, looking at an architectural magazine from her coffee table.

He looked so…*right*, sitting there. Relaxed and at home, incredibly masculine. And for the moment, all hers.

What was she worried about?

She'd uncorked the wine in the kitchen and brought two glasses with her, setting them on the table, noting he'd pulled the curtains. She filled one of the glasses and turned to him.

He put down the magazine, offering a curious look at the single glass.

She bit her lip, jumping in and convincing herself to take this chance to explore some fantasies, perhaps.

Handing him the glass, she didn't sit next to him,

but instead lowered down over his lap, straddling his strong thighs and enjoying the flicker of surprise—and approval—in his expression.

Della took the glass from his hand, dipped her finger into the bright, golden wine and traced it over his lips.

Heat sparked in his eyes, and she was relieved again that she hadn't spoiled the evening. Leaning down to lick it from his mouth, she was surprised to feel him catch his breath.

So she did it again, though this time he caught her finger in between his lips and sucked the taste from her skin, and it was her turn to gasp at the incredible sensation.

She knew that fingertips were one of the most concentrated nerve centers in the body, but she'd never really considered them an erogenous zone before—until Gabe sucked in her finger a second time, sending a shock of pleasure down between her thighs, which tightened and squeezed his.

Gabe noticed. "Do it again."

She did, dipping her fingers into the wine and then to his mouth, and the same sensation made her shudder, her eyes closing.

"It's, um, been a while," she managed, breathless. "I guess I'm extra sensitive."

"Well, that makes this even more fun," he said, taking the wineglass from her and setting it on the table next to the magazines.

He didn't take his eyes from hers as he slid his fingers up under her tank top, lifting it up over her head. Then he removed her bra and gazed at her breasts with raw hunger in his eyes.

"Gorgeous," he said roughly and took the glass of

wine again, now wetting his fingers with the Riesling and tracing the wet, cold wine around one nipple, making her whimper. He licked it off and then he did the same to her other breast.

"Oh, yes," she panted, tightening her thighs on his.

"More?"

"Please."

He repeated the process until Della was so close to the edge of orgasm that she could only brace herself on his shoulders and focus on all of the sensations, but it wasn't quite enough.

Until he put the wine down, and while still kissing her breasts he began to gently rub the heel of his hand between her legs.

Seconds later, she was crying out in a voice that didn't sound like herself at all, the quick rush of satisfaction both offering some relief, but also making her hungrier.

Gabe pulled back, his eyes bright, his jaw taut with arousal. Looking down, Della saw more evidence of that, and smiled, pride surging through her.

She'd done that. To a man like Gabe.

What else could she do?

She drew her tongue along the strong cords of his neck and let one hand slip down to investigate that prominent evidence of his own excitement.

He growled, or groaned, a purely masculine expression of desire as she touched him, pressing her fingers over him through the fabric of his slacks. He turned his head, taking her mouth in a hot kiss that threw fuel on the fire inside of her. This time, touching wouldn't be enough.

"You need to get those pants off." Her voice sounded

strange to her, breathless and urgent, saying those words so boldly.

"I agree," Gabe said as she moved off of him, finding her knees slightly shaky as she stood in the middle of her apartment. It was surreal, watching him undress. He peeled off his clothes without preamble or self-consciousness, throwing them on the plush floral rug, and his shirt landed over a chair across from her. Taking her cue from him, Della peeled off her skirt and panties, and then they were both standing there naked in her living room.

It went far beyond any fantasy she'd had on the plane, or, well, ever. This moment with Gabe, looking at his strong, lean form, the impressive erection that jutted out from his thighs and the intensity in his face as he studied her—it was a memory meant for a lifetime.

He closed the distance between them in two easy steps, pulling her up close, flush against him. She was more than a foot shorter than him, so her face cradled against his pectorals, his shaft at her waist. She turned her head, rubbing her skin against the light sprinkling of hair, and darted her tongue out to taste him.

"Della," he said, his tone a mix of protest and a need so thick in his voice that he didn't sound quite the same, either. "Wait," he said, letting her go so he could retrieve an item from his wallet, quickly covering himself. She couldn't take her eyes off of him, watching and absorbing every erotic detail.

She raised her eyes to his and he smiled.

"There are other things I want to do to you, lovely Della, so many things. But for now, I think we both need this," he whispered as he lifted her in his arms as if she weighed nothing. "I fantasized about you like this, being inside of you, all of that time on the plane," he added as she wrapped her arms and legs around him.

"Really?" she squeaked as he put his hands on her backside, holding her in place.

"Really."

The way he was holding her, she felt him, the thick weight of him against her inner thigh, then prodding against her entrance.

"Okay?"

"Oh yes," she said softly against his ear, then nipped the lobe.

Her arms tightened around his neck as he pressed slowly inside, letting her take him bit by bit. Her forehead fell to his shoulder as he filled her. The delightful pressure drew a sigh from her as she closed her eyes, trying to feel it all. The sensation was overwhelming, and she wanted to simply bask in it, until he spoke, his voice rough.

"Kiss me, Della."

She fluttered light touches over his mouth with hers, and then settled in, slower, deeper. Sucking his tongue between her lips, she enjoyed his taste. He started moving, bracing her in his hands as he thrust lightly. She moaned, her head falling back.

"Keep kissing me, don't stop."

Della wasn't sure she could do it, the increasing friction and pace of his thrusts blanking her mind and taking her higher, but she did keep kissing him.

She framed his face with her hands, drawing back from the kisses as pleasure spiked. She couldn't do anything but look in his eyes as her entire body was taken over, the pleasure rippling through every nerve ending, leaving her helpless to do anything but ride it out.

Seconds later, he took her mouth in a wet, hot kiss and groaned so deeply that she could feel the vibrations of the sound all through her. Her arms latched around him as he gave in to his own release, and miraculously triggered another intense, quick climax for her, too.

As his movements slowed, only their ragged breathing and gasps filled the space. Della was still holding on, though they were both slick with sweat, their bodies still clinging, still connected.

"Oh my," she breathed against his skin, unsure she could stand on her own if he let her go.

He knew, and took her to the sofa, setting her down slowly, and then he sat, too, pulling her alongside him, cuddled against his chest.

"You are...incredible."

"Me? I just hung on. You were the incredible one," she said, smiling against his side.

"It's like I told you on the plane. We're great together. I had a feeling we would be. I'm glad we had the chance to find out."

Della paused, her mind clearing somewhat.

"That sounds like a goodbye," she said.

He tipped her chin up with his fingers, looking down at her. "Not yet. The night is young, and like I said, there are a lot of things I want to do to you, Della."

Happiness surged and she bit her lip, flirting up at him from beneath her lashes.

"There are a few things I'd like to do to you, too."

"I can't wait to find out. But maybe a shower first?"

She nodded, her imagination swimming with the

possibilities of what they could do to each other under the hot water.

"That sounds like fun," she responded with a smile, standing and holding out her hand to him.

He followed her down the hall, and Della smiled secretly to herself, thinking that this was what she had been looking for. The blow-your-mind kind of sex that everyone talked about. She had finally experienced it, and now she was about to experience some more of it.

In fact, she wanted to enjoy as much sex with Gabe as humanly possible before he left, because she had a feeling this was going to be a one-night thing.

Taking his hand as she pulled him into the shower stall, she turned on the water and sank to her knees before him, fully intending to live every single fantasy she could, while she had the chance.

3

GABE WASN'T PROUD of himself as he snuck around Della's house while she slept, but it was a necessary evil. After she passed out, he extricated himself from her arms and went downstairs for a more thorough look through her office and then returned upstairs. She was still asleep in the bed, naked, exhausted and wrapped around the tumbled sheets in such a sexy way that he thought about waking her up again. But he wasn't done.

He slid his fingers along the edges of the built-in bookcases, a small flashlight held between his teeth as he noticed books on just about everything. A good deal of fiction, but also science, math, art and, more unexpectedly, sex.

Several books on the art of lovemaking and the biology of pleasure, he noted with a raised eyebrow.

Well, from his experience, she'd definitely done her research. She wasn't terribly experienced, he could tell, but she was eager and imaginative. That was preferable, in his book.

He studied the arrangement of the books, looking for anything odd or out of place, something that had been turned differently or was misplaced, but found nothing. No bugs, nothing that would suggest she had been compromised in any way.

Except by him.

He investigated the lamps, her clock, the vents... anyplace someone might hide a camera or a microphone, but there was nothing.

Gabe was happy about that, for several reasons. He shouldn't have been *happy*, but there was undeniable relief that Della appeared to have no involvement in his current investigation.

Though he still had to go through the locked files on her computer.

He understood now why she had balked when he'd asked to be taken upstairs earlier in the evening. This part of her home was clearly her private space. The entire home was lovely, but this was the place where she truly escaped.

A huge four-poster bed, very feminine and wickedly comfortable, dominated the room. It had been tough for him to stay awake, waiting for her to drift off.

The white cotton frills that rimmed the canopy were balanced by plain wool rugs and simple furniture that gave the room a Zen feeling. Built-in bookcases lined one wall, and there was an easel near a pair of French doors that led out to a terrace. A half-finished watercolor—amateurish, but still charming—sat on the perch. She was painting the view from her veranda, it seemed. And what might have been a bird, but it was hard to tell, exactly.

"Gabe?" Her sleepy voice suddenly interrupted his thoughts, and he switched off the flashlight quickly, leaving it on the dresser, where he'd found it as he went back to the bed.

"Did I wake you up? Sorry. I was trying to be quiet."

"What are you doing?"

As he approached the bed, his cock twitched with interest. Incredible, after the mini-marathon they'd enjoyed. He hadn't been this interested in a woman for some time.

"Just looking for my clothes."

"They're downstairs," she said on a yawn.

"Oh right," he feigned, knowing that, but needing to come up with some excuse in case she'd noticed him hunting around her room.

"You're leaving?"

"I have to. I shouldn't have stayed this late. Early morning."

"Oh. Okay," she said, sounding mildly disappointed, but accepting. "I'll walk you down."

"No need for that."

"I want to. I'm awake anyway."

She slid out of bed, and he could see the contours of her shape in the sliver of light peeking in through a curtain.

He hardened, and had to keep himself from touching, his mind scrambling to stem his reaction. He usually had much better control over himself than this.

Della switched on a low light and took her robe from the chair near the bookshelves. How could she look even sexier putting something *on*?

Her mouth was still swollen from their kissing, but her lips turned down slightly at the edges. Her hair was tumbled everywhere around her face from how he'd combed his fingers through it while pressing her down into the mattress. He looked away. Della was far too tempting.

He slid a look as she bent down to pick up something from the floor, the edge of the robe riding up to the edge of her upper thigh. He groaned, crossing to where she stood and sliding his hands over the soft roundness of her backside. He pushed the robe up, nudged his erection against her bottom and heard her catch her breath.

"Maybe I could stay a bit longer," he said, giving in as she rose and leaned back against him.

She turned to him with a sigh. She planted her hands on his chest and shook her head.

"We can't. No more protection."

He was truly disappointed, but slid his arm around the small of her back and tugged her closer, not willing to give up entirely.

Burying his face in the soft skin of her neck, he licked the spot behind her ear and felt her shudder.

She was sensitive all over, loving to be touched. That made him want to do it even more.

"Gabe, we—"

"Have options," he said with a chuckle, and kissed a path down to her breast, sucking the sweet flesh there in between his lips as his hands delved lower.

She was already hot, wet, and cried out, gripping his shoulders the minute his fingers found her.

He slipped her hand inside his boxers to stoke his erection, showing her the rhythm he liked. And then he turned all of his attention to kissing every soft spot he could find as they stroked and brought each other to another slow, incredible climax. Gabe thought his knees might actually be slightly shaky; he knew hers were as she sagged against him.

"You are one sexy lady, Della Clark," he said on a breathless chuckle.

She sighed and buried her face in his chest, nuzzling there. He let her, enjoying that moment, but gently disentangled himself a few minutes later.

"I do have to go."

She looked at him, sleepy and satisfied, and nodded. "I know."

After a quick wash in her en suite, which nearly had them all over each other again, they walked downstairs together.

Gabe couldn't help but feel mildly regretful that he had to leave. He imagined waking up next to Della would be fun. There were so many ways he could rouse her in the morning.

He stopped short for a second. He never had thoughts like that with other women he'd slept with. Never had a problem leaving after the moment had passed. As he plucked his clothes from the floor and the coffee table where he'd thrown them earlier, he realized he didn't really want to say goodbye. He wanted to see her again.

That didn't happen often, either. But Della was…different. She leaned on the doorjamb between the living room and the entryway, watching him, looking sleepy, and maybe a bit sad.

Or was Gabe imagining that? Wishful thinking?

Once he was dressed, he planted his hands on his hips, took a breath, his resolve returning.

"I should get some sleep," she said, clearly trying

to avoid the awkward goodbye. "Thank you. I hope you…have a nice stay in the city."

"Della, wait."

He walked toward her and drew her into a hug, kissed her hair, then her cheek and her lips, before he backed away.

"Thank you," he whispered.

Her lips parted like she was going to say something, but no words came out, so he walked to the door, stepping out into the early morning darkness. The upper Manhattan streets were quiet. There wasn't a cab in sight, so Gabe headed to the nearest subway station, refocusing on his task and leaving Della's welcoming warmth behind.

DELLA DIDN'T HEAR the conversation going on around her, she was too busy thinking about randomness. The odds of her meeting Gabe were, in the context of the entire world, astronomical. If he hadn't been seated next to her, would the night before have even happened? Would they have met by some other mechanism? Would she have tripped over his foot in the aisle on her way to the bathrooms, and he might have caught her? Or would they still have mixed up their bags?

No, her analytical mind rebelled. That would suggest fate or determinism. That they were "meant to be." That was romantic nonsense, according to her mathematician's mind. It was impossible to know how they ended up sitting next to each other, only that they did. If she had more data, such as when they had bought tickets, how many seats were gone at the time and a swath of other information, she could figure out the probabilities. Then their ending up together would seem far less magical.

But the night they'd spent together *had* been magic. Chemistry, not physics.

"Della? Della, what do you think? What do you have there?"

Chloe Brown, her colleague and friend, marched across the carpeted floor of the fancy dressing room to pluck a napkin from Della's fingers that had been under her champagne glass. The ladies she had been chatting with walked back out into the main area of the store, no doubt to retrieve more dresses.

Chloe's huge blue eyes widened as she glanced at the paper in her hand.

"Math? You're doing *math*? I need opinions on this dress, and then we need to get your dress, as well. The wedding is in three weeks, you know." Chloe sighed. "I must have been out of my mind to agree to such a rushed date, but with Justin's job moving, we couldn't wait."

"I'm sorry. I know I'm supposed to be the one supporting *you*, but I'm just distracted today," Della apologized.

She *should* be focusing more on the dress choices and helping Chloe, but all she seemed to be able to think about was what happened with Gabe last night.

Chloe looked at the napkin more closely.

"Wait a minute…what's that graph? Who's *Gabe*?"

Della had forgotten that she'd labeled her variables with G and D, and reached to snatch the slip of paper from Chloe's hands.

"Nuh-uh. Come to think of it, you were late this morning, and you're never late. You have shadows under your eyes, like you didn't sleep well. And what's that red mark behind your ear…is that a *hickey*?"

Della scrunched her shoulders, hiding the mark, and inwardly chastising herself for not wearing a scarf, but it was summer in New York—wearing a scarf would draw even more attention.

"What are you, a detective?" Della grumbled, sticking her tongue out, but having a tough time hiding a smile.

She, Della Clark, had girl talk to share.

How many times had she sat at lunch or out for drinks, listening to friends talk about their dates, man troubles and sex lives, when she had nothing to contribute. Now she did.

But she was finding it hard to talk about her news, surprisingly.

What would Chloe think of her? She was marrying a guy she'd been with for years, since college. And Della had taken a man she met on the plane to her apartment for a night of amazing sex.

And she wished she could do it again. Maybe that was the problem with her dating life. She was looking for Mr. Right instead of Mr. Right Now. If she wanted great sex, did she really need a relationship?

Chloe plopped down in the large, cushiony chair next to Della, the satin and lace of the dress she wore billowing all around her. Della reached out and took one edge of the lovely fabric between her fingers, marveling at how soft it was and how detailed the design of the lace.

"It almost looks like fractals," Della murmured, studying the design.

Was she really only interested in one-time sex? It

satisfied a short-term goal, for sure, but what about longer-term goals? What about a day when she might get to wear a dress like this? Have children? Grow old with someone?

What if she missed meeting the man she could spend the rest of her life with when she was pursuing simple pleasure? Not that any of her dating profile responses today looked any more promising than before on either score.

"Della, honey, tell me what happened," Chloe said, breaking into her thoughts and taking Della's hand with a friendly squeeze.

"I don't know if I made a mistake. But it's made me rethink everything," Della said. "I'm a little confused."

Once she started telling Chloe about Gabe, and what had happened, it all poured out much more easily than she thought it would. Chloe listened, and when Della was finally finished explaining as much as she could—without certain details, of course—she saw her friend was smiling.

"Well. Good for you, Della. It's about time."

Della sat back in the chair, surprised. "You don't think I'm a...well, a slut?"

Chloe burst out laughing. "No, not at all. It sounds to me like you met a great guy and had a good time. No harm in that. I slept with Justin the first night we met, too. And had fun with quite a few men I knew before him. There's nothing wrong with sex for fun."

"Really?"

"Really. Who knows, a one-night stand could be your wedding-dress guy someday. Stranger things happen. People meet in all kinds of ways."

"I just wish... I'd really like to see him again. Gabe.

I feel like last night was kind of a dream, and believe me, the odds of me finding another man like him are not high."

"Well, why don't you see him again?"

"Our meeting was totally random and totally random things are not repeatable," Della said, and then saw that look on her friend's face.

"This has nothing to do with math, Della. What's really going on?"

"He made it clear it was just a one-night thing. He's only here for a short time, works with the government, something with Homeland Security. When he left, he didn't say he wanted to see me again. Or what if I did, and it wasn't as good? Maybe last night was just a fluke."

Chloe paused, sitting back in her chair. "There's only one way to find out. You contacted him once about your bags, just contact him again. You don't have to wait for him to ask, Della. You can ask for what you want, and you should."

Della frowned. "I don't know, I feel weird calling him again. Especially for, um, you know for—"

"For sex. Believe me, he won't mind," Chloe said with a chuckle. "The worst that can happen is that he says no, or doesn't pick up the call. Then you have your answer."

Della shook her head. "And if he says yes, what if I miss my chance at someone else really great?"

"By the looks of the responses you have on your dating profile, I don't think you have to worry about that anytime soon. If you want to see this guy again, you need to go for it."

Della was tempted, but not convinced. She'd worked

with men her entire life, and she was used to being the
only woman in the room many times when it came
to lectures or think tanks, but this was different. She
would feel so foolish if he said no, and that would put
a pall on the entire experience. Wouldn't it be better
just to enjoy the memory?

No, she was just making excuses.

"Think of it this way. It's practice, right? You
haven't had a lot of chances to be with men who really know what they're doing, and now you met one.
Enjoy it, work off some steam and get some mad skills
in bed for when you do meet Mr. Forever."

Della brightened slightly. "That's true."

"And if he's working for DHS, he has to be pretty
trustworthy, right? What kind of work does he do for
them? Is there some kind of problem in the city? Some
new threat?"

Chloe looked slightly worried suddenly.

"Oh no, nothing like that," Della reassured. "I'm
sure he wouldn't be hooking up with me if it was anything that serious. But we didn't really talk about work
that much."

"If you must calculate odds, the best bet is that if
you meet him again, you'll have a great time. A guy
that good in bed doesn't lose his skills overnight, so
take advantage while you can. Anything else, you can't
know for sure, no matter how many algorithms you
apply."

Della realized Chloe was right. It was her downfall
that she often made things more complicated rather
than simplifying them. Divide, instead of multiply. Just
call Gabe and see what happened, and no matter what

happened, she would have made a decision. It was better than drowning in what-ifs.

"You're right. I feel so much better. I'll call him after we're done here," she said, excitement making her bounce in her seat.

"Great! Maybe we could even do a double date, or if he's here for a while, he could be your wedding date, perhaps?"

"Let's see if he even talks to me. I don't want to count on anything."

Chloe smiled. "Now you're learning. Just enjoy the moment. But still, if there's a chance, I'd love to meet him. He sounds like quite a guy."

Della smiled in return. "That would be nice. Thanks, Chloe."

"You're welcome. Now, what do you think of this dress? It's the one I keep coming back to, but the cost is through the roof."

Chloe stood, and Della, having made her decision to call Gabe and take control of her destiny—or at least of her sex life—was able to focus on the task at hand. She followed her friend to the mirror, studying how lovely Chloe looked in the gown. The special moment settled in, and tears burned at the back of her eyes, but she blinked them away.

"I love it. It's perfect. You only get married once, Chloe, and you should have the dress you dream about."

Chloe looked like she was blinking away tears as well, and nodded.

"You have a romantic streak, Della. And it's so good to have you here. I know we've known each other for less than a year, and this wedding was sort of a rush, but you've been such a good friend. And with none of my own family around, you've really become more like a sister."

Now Della did get teary, as she had no siblings, either. To think that Chloe felt that way about her was very moving.

"Thank you. I feel exactly the same. I'm so honored that you asked me to be your maid of honor, even though you know I have no clue what I'm doing."

They laughed, and Chloe grinned. "How are the dance lessons coming along?"

Della made a face. "I suck."

Chloe laughed again. "You're being too hard on yourself. You haven't had much time to learn. And you need a good partner. Maybe Gabe can help you out," she added with a hint of mischief.

Della bit her lip, wondering. She hadn't considered that, or that perhaps Gabe would be her date to some wedding events, if he was around. Justin's best man was married, so Della had resigned herself to going solo, but maybe...?

Don't go there, she reminded herself. That way lay disappointment. Just enjoy whatever happens, if anything does happen.

"So, now that we know what I'm wearing to this event, we need to try on your selections."

"Selections? I haven't made any selections yet."

"I did," Chloe said mischievously.

Della rolled her eyes, but submitted as Chloe signaled to the saleslady to bring in some of the dresses she had set aside for Della.

Chloe was always chiding her about her bland style, wearing mostly black and grey, wool and cotton, and relatively modest clothes. The skirt and tank top she'd worn out with Gabe the night before had been obtained on a shopping trip with Chloe, who had given in on the black tank top, but convinced her to buy the form-fitting denim skirt.

Gabe had clearly approved, and so Della decided maybe Chloe had a point.

The saleslady brought in three dresses, and all of them made Della gasp.

"Gorgeous, aren't they?" Chloe cooed. "C'mon, try them on."

Della was led away by the saleswoman, along with the gowns. The assortment ranged among shades of rose, which was Chloe's choice, of course, and all three were as daring as they were…sensual.

The first one was a Grecian, off-the-shoulder style of sheer, draped material that caught at the waist with a silver pin. It moved around her in the most wonderful froth of fabric Della had ever imagined. When she walked, it was if she were floating.

"Oh, that one is superb. It would drive any man crazy," Chloe said approvingly.

"It's very comfortable, too. I like it."

"Try the next, anyway. We need to see all of them."

Grudgingly, she did so. The second one had a neckline so deep Della was pretty sure she could probably step out of the dress through the front. Chloe liked it, but commented that Della would probably have to tape her breasts in place, so as not to have a fashion faux pas. Della nixed that dress immediately.

The third was more modestly cut, but fit like a glove, and because of that, was even more revealing than the others.

"I like it," Della said, studying her image in the

mirror with Chloe. She looked so sleek, and the dress seemed to compress all of her curves into a very nice shape. "But it doesn't feel as nice as the first one, and it would be difficult to dance in this one. I really like the Grecian style, and I would rather move comfortably."

"Agreed. And the first is a very romantic dress, while still being sexy. It also looked the best with your hair color and figure. I was worried that rose color, with your strawberry, would be a clash, but that shade works. I think because it's muted, and the off-the-shoulder style takes the color away from your neckline, so it shows off that amazing skin of yours, rather than clashing with your hair."

Della smirked. "You really think a lot about these kinds of things. Good thing one of us does."

Chloe chuckled. "You have basically good instincts. You just need to be a bit more daring."

"So this is decided?"

"Yes. Do you want to go get a coffee to celebrate?"

"I can't," Della said, looking at her watch. "I wanted to drop some paperwork off downtown, and I have an appointment after that."

"And you have to call lover boy."

Della felt her cheeks warm. "Yes, and that."

"Speaking of that, maybe you should buy some sexy extras while you're here. They have some beautiful things out front."

"Oh, I don't know—"

"Don't second-guess, Della. You're having a fling with a sexy stranger. Make the most of it."

Della took a deep breath and agreed with a nod. Returning to the dressing room, she took the dress off, and then waited for the store's seamstress to take her measurements so that it could be altered appropriately.

Then, she and Chloe bought several more pieces of lingerie than Della thought she would ever need, but they were fun to pick out. She wondered if Gabe would be surprised. Last night, all she had been wearing were her usual, plain cotton bikinis and he hadn't seemed to mind at all.

Leaving the shop, she and Chloe parted ways, and Della's attention turned to the evening ahead. She was too distracted to think about work, and it wasn't anything that couldn't wait.

Chloe was right—she had to go for it with Gabe. She had everything to gain, and very little to lose. But she balked at calling him and suggesting he come to her house. Should they meet somewhere else?

If she asked him out for a drink, and then things happened more naturally, she was far more comfortable with that.

But that was also *boring*.

Della was tired of being boring. Gabe was a federal agent, and a man who had experienced a lot more of life than she had. What made her think he would want to see her again? She wanted to stand out in his memory like he did in hers. To make herself desirable, more mysterious.

Maybe if she did something more creative than just calling him—she could make it a game of sorts.

Excitement tingled underneath her skin as an idea formed, and before she could talk herself out of it, she took out her phone and opened the GPS application. Some quick calculations, and she'd sent off a message

to Gabe that hopefully would be much more intrigu-
ing than a phone call would have been.

Putting her phone away, she hurried down the sidewalk, smiling. She had more plans to make.

4

GABE FINISHED HIS second drink, looking at the door of the Wall Street bar where he'd agreed to meet Della. Well, he assumed that was what this was about. All he'd received from her was a message that included GPS coordinates that led to this location. At first he'd been suspicious—what if it wasn't her? Or why wouldn't she just call him directly?

Gabe became increasingly antsy and curious the longer he sat, waiting.

What was Della up to?

He wasn't sure he should be here, or if he should have made any plans to see her again at all. He'd combed through her locked files and found nothing of too much interest. Her work on the vaccine project had been mostly related to risk analysis, very compartmentalized and early in the project. There were no other red flags in her life. Her emails and academic work were all straightforward. He was running background checks on her friends, colleagues, just in case, but there'd been nothing overtly alarming.

He shouldn't have come here, but the strange message had intrigued him. If it wasn't from Della, then he needed to know what was going on.

Right.

The truth was that he liked her, and he wanted to see her again, in spite of the situation.

You lied to her, so what? It's the job. Lives depend on what you do. His mind replayed all the usual things he told himself so he could sleep at night. It wasn't that they weren't true, but they were getting harder and harder to believe.

Like today, which he'd spent interrogating a twenty-five-year-old junior scientist about the details of her private life until she was in tears. Tears never really bothered him; Gabe knew they could be a ploy. There had been enough cracks in the young employee's interview to push her harder, and questions about her background, as well. Natalie Petroski could be the leak. He'd asked for surveillance to be installed in her home before she returned there.

Until they were satisfied that she was clean, he would review audio and video of everything she did, every aspect of her personal life, and with whom she did it. Especially with whom. They'd have to get some mobile surveillance on her as well, know where she went and who she saw.

It was legal—he had authorization—but it made Gabe feel dirty. And undeserving, he supposed, of spending time with someone like Della. What would she think if she knew?

He shook his head in disgust; he was getting soft. He never would have thought this way before.

Before what? Before deceiving too many people, losing too many friends and spending too many lonely nights thinking about it? Before he let himself love someone, thinking there was a future in it, only to find out differently? Before he let someone count more than the job, and it cost him his life? Or theirs?

He couldn't deny it; since Janet had died, he'd started having doubts. He told himself it was grief, or a broken heart, but those things passed.

His doubts remained.

Maybe Della was a mistake for a whole different set of reasons. He had to focus on his work, and she was a distraction. A sexy distraction, but one he couldn't afford. He'd often wondered on sleepless nights, if doubts about him, or about her choices, had been what distracted Janet. If they had created enough of a crack that she missed the shooter who hadn't missed her. Had she thought of him in the end?

He shook his head as if trying to ward off the bad memories. He walked to the door, intending to leave as he saw a guy on a bike race to a stop in front. The man hopped off of the bike and then came through the door. He looked right at Gabe.

"This is for you."

The guy handed him a small white box, wrapped with a black bow.

"Who sent it?"

Gabe was hardwired against receiving any mysterious packages, and automatically backed up as he assessed the situation around him.

"A really hot redhead," the kid said with a large grin. "Lucky you."

Gabe released a breath, the tension easing from his shoulders as he took the box and tipped the delivery guy, who sped off, leaving him standing there in the doorway to the bar, staring at the box.

Even knowing it was probably from Della, and all was probably fine, he had to fight every instinct in his mind to actually pull the ribbon and open the box. This didn't seem like something the woman he'd met would do—she wasn't the type.

His eyes widened as he lifted a sheer stocking from the box. Attached to the stocking was a piece of paper.

"What the...?"

Detaching the paper, he put the stocking back in the box and studied the numbers on the sheet of paper. It was definitely Della's handwriting. He recognized it from all of the papers he'd gone through in her computer bag.

He took a seat at the bar, studying the sheet.

What was she up to?

After a minute or two, he saw the start of the pattern, discerning the code. His heartbeat sped up a little—Della was luring him to her with a system of clues.

Or was it some kind of trap?

Grabbing a pen from his pocket, he worked out the clues in a matter of minutes. The numbers were a subway line, an address and a time signature—he should be at the location indicated by eight.

That gave him about a half hour to make it all the way uptown. Apparently, this train would get him there on time.

Booking it to the closest subway platform, he boarded the train, which he had nearly missed.

What was Della up to? Where was she leading him?

Sitting down on an empty bench, he opened the box

again and touched the soft material of the stocking, his blood instantly warming.

The idea of being with Della again was intoxicating, and this game was making it even more so.

Apparently there was more to Dr. Clark than he'd assumed. If she was trying to draw him in, it was working. Though Gabe still kept his guard up—he couldn't be sure this was really Della or that there wasn't something else going on.

Eventually, he emerged onto the street, and the signs near the subway platform told him he was near the American Museum of Natural History.

He stood there for a while, looking for another clue and checking his watch. Eight on the dot, but no Della in sight.

Then he saw it—a napkin from the Italian restaurant they'd eaten at the night they met, tacked to the telephone pole at the corner.

He quickly took it from the pole and saw Della's script again. She'd written only *I'm waiting for you under the stars.*

The stars? It was not quite dark yet, though the stars were peeking out a few places, he noticed, looking up.

Then his eye caught sight of a sign pointing to the natural history museum, which contained the Hayden Planetarium. Following the signs to the museum, he saw it was closed.

What was he supposed to do now?

"Are you Gabe Ross?" someone asked.

Gabe spun around to find a small, compact woman staring at him—her uniform said she was museum security.

"I am."

"Della told me you were a tall drink of water," she said with a grin. "Follow me, please."

They went in a side door, through a warehouse and then upstairs to the main entry.

"She's waiting for you in her favorite spot," the guard said, pointing to a sign. "Just follow those signs, and you'll find her. And no rush, I'm here all night," she said with a wink before turning back the other way.

Gabe followed her directions, and soon the beautiful astronomy exhibit came into view, a globe in a huge transparent room. He looked around, but didn't see Della. Then he noticed the door was open to the actual planetarium, and he went inside.

Slowly. Cautiously. His hand on his sidearm, just in case.

But then he saw her.

She was down on the floor by the stage, the only one in the glowing light of the room, stars floating by on the massive screen overhead.

"Della?"

He walked down to find her stretched out on the floor on a plaid blanket, staring upward, the bottle of wine and some snacks in a basket by the corner of the blanket.

Her eyes met his. "Gabe. You came."

He lowered himself down to the blanket. "What's this all about, Della?"

She sat up, smiling at him.

Gabe could only stare at how pretty she was, completely distracted as the soft starlight fell over her face and burnished curls.

"Do you have my stocking?"

He blinked, then realized she meant the one in the box.

"Yeah."

She took it and unfolded one leg from underneath her, reaching to slide the sheer piece of cloth over her foot and calf.

Gabe's mouth went dry as he watched.

"Della—"

She put her hand gently on top of his. For all of her seductive play, her expression seemed unsure, her touch tentative.

"I hoped you'd come, but I wasn't certain. I wanted to see you again, but I also wanted it to be special. Memorable."

Gabe nodded. "You managed that. You're full of surprises, Della."

She grinned. "Isn't it gorgeous? It's the sky, what it looked like two million years ago."

He looked up. "It's pretty impressive."

Gabe loosened his tie, leaned back on his elbow. He wasn't as interested in looking at the sky projection as he was looking at Della.

How was it that she seemed to be more beautiful than the last time he saw her?

"So do you know any of the stars or constellations?"

"Not really. I know the basics—Big Dipper, Orion, the stuff you learn in grade school."

"Not an astronomy geek?"

"Nope, just a math geek, which is more than geeky enough, believe me," she said with a sigh. "Sometimes you can know too much, and my father told me that some things should stay magical. I love watching the stars, looking at flowers. I don't need to know how they work, or all of the details. They're just beautiful."

He reached for her hand, held it in his, feeling the

mood shift, the world narrowing down to just the two of them.

"I can understand that. Knowing too much—about anything—definitely can make you jaded. It's nice that you want to keep some things sacred."

She smiled, squeezing his hand. "Thank you."

"And you are the least geeky person I know—especially in that dress and those heels. Definitely not geeky."

Her eyes lowered, lashes brushing her cheek, but he could tell she was pleased.

His heart stuttered slightly as he watched her lips part, and he knew he was going down a dangerous path.

"I almost didn't come tonight," he blurted.

Her head shot up and she looked at him in surprise.

"Why not?"

"I wasn't sure if I should. I wasn't completely honest with you, Della. I do work in logistics, but I also do more. The kind of things I can't tell you about."

Her brow rose slightly, and she nodded, seeming to understand.

"My job has jaded me, Della. I wasn't even sure about your clues, the package, the note. I thought it might be some kind of a trick, or a trap," he said, shaking his head and exhaling a deep breath. "I'm not an easy man, Della. And I tend to think the worst. It comes with the job."

"Oh," she said, her hand coming to her lips as her eyes widened in realization. "I'm so sorry—I didn't even think how you might see this as suspicious—"

He put his hand up, stemming her apologies.

"There was no reason for you to. Normal people wouldn't see it that way. But my life…it's how my mind works, I guess. I don't believe in romance, or magic, or…this," he said, looking up at the stars. "I can't afford to."

"Why not?" she said, her lips dipping into a small frown.

"It's a distraction. *You're* a distraction, and that can be dangerous."

Gabe hadn't intended to put everything out on the table like that, but it was incredibly good to be able to say something openly and honestly, and he hadn't said anything that would compromise his case.

Della looked at him, dumbstruck. "I'm a distraction?"

"A big one. It took me a while to stop thinking about last night. But the things I have to do, Della, sometimes… I don't think you'd want to be with me if you knew."

He hadn't talked to anyone about his work in so long, on a personal level, that he didn't realize how much he'd needed to. He and Janet had talked, but it was different, since they were partners. When they became intimate, they tried to leave work behind, though it was almost impossible. It was too much a part of who they were.

To be able to say something he was feeling, even if in a roundabout way, was enormous. It was possible that he would put off Della by admitting so much, but maybe that would be a good thing.

She was quiet for several beats, and then met his look with a steady one of her own.

"I may not know about your work specifically, and I understand why you can't tell me, but I can guess. I know the costs, as well. It doesn't mean you're a bad

person, or that you don't have a right to have a life.
Maybe you need those moments of magic more than
anyone."

"I appreciate that, but I don't think you really can
know—"

"I do. I do have security clearance—not as high as
yours, I imagine, but high enough that I've worked with
people in your position from time to time, and I see the
toll it takes. One analyst I worked with on a project in
DC, he killed himself after he made a wrong call on a
project. It wasn't his fault, not really. There were other
people who could have caught the mistake, too, but he
couldn't live with it. So, I do know."

He was aware she had clearance, and he was aware
of the incident she mentioned, but her empathy was
probably the most surprising thing to him of all. There
wasn't much of that in his world, not unless you were
using it to get something you wanted. Everything in
his world was strategic, an angle. Even magic.

Like a magician on stage, his life was made of illu-
sions and sleight of hand. It was just another thing to
use to get what you needed, he thought darkly.

What did he need from Della? Why was he here?
He should stay as far away from her as he could, but
he couldn't quite convince himself of that.

"I'm sorry that happened to you," he offered. "It's
terrible. I've seen too many people—friends, colleagues—who lost their lives, or ended up coping in
self-destructive ways."

He took a sip of his wine, looking away. He was
going down a road he would rather avoid. What was
it about Della?

"Thanks for sharing with me. I had doubts, too, believe me. I came up with the game idea because I didn't have the nerve to call you. If you hadn't shown up tonight, I could have saved some face, I guess."

"I wouldn't have said no, if you had called."

"Chloe said I need to take control of my fate, to ask for what I want, go after it. I've always been good at that professionally. Not so much on a personal level," she confessed, taking a deep drink of her wine.

"Hmm. Why don't you tell me now? Tell me what you want," he said, dropping his voice, changing the tone of their conversation to a different kind of intimacy. One he could handle much more easily.

She started to say something, then stopped. Her expression was intrigued, but reluctant. Shy. Gabe wanted to show her, again, how sexy she was.

"How much privacy do we have here, Della?" He leaned in to kiss a spot behind her ear that he knew drove her wild. Her breath caught and a tremble that moved through her limbs was his reward.

"Lock that main door and we're completely alone for as long as we want to be."

It was exactly what Gabe wanted to hear.

DELLA STOOD WATCHING as Gabe jogged up the aisle to close the door and then turned back, slipping off his loosened tie as he returned. She was rooted to the spot, her entire being vibrating in anticipation, desire thrumming through her, wiping out any vestige of exhaustion or tension from the day.

He threw his tie on the blanket, and his coat, too. Then he rejoined her, sliding his hand up into her hair, cradling her head gently as his eyes moved over her face.

"What do you want, Della?" he repeated.

Everything, she thought. Her imagination was wading into perilous waters, the ones that existed far past "just sex." She had no business there.

"Kiss me."

He pulled her into his arms, kissing her like his life depended on it. Her need met his on exactly the same level, returning his passion with all of her own. As if he had been as hungry for her as she was for him.

"I want to touch you," she said against his mouth, finding the second request easier.

His arms left her, and he started unbuttoning his shirt, but she stopped him.

"Let me," she said, planting a soft kiss at the base of his throat as she pushed his fingers away and worked the buttons herself, removing the dress shirt from his shoulders. She loved the masculine look of the white T-shirt he wore underneath. The soft cotton teased the backs of her fingers as she slid her hand up underneath it, making him groan and his muscles tense.

She lightly drew her nails down his chest, experimenting, watching his reactions. It *was* magic, she thought as she noticed the pulse in his throat, to make a man's heart beat so quickly with only a touch.

"You make me lose my mind, Della, with one kiss, one touch."

Peering up at him from under her lashes she smiled. "I'm glad I'm not the only one."

Bolder, she pushed the shirt up over his head and then trailed kisses down his pectorals. Then the tip of her tongue landed along the light trail of hair that led to the band of his trousers. When she unbuttoned them, and let the back of her hand run along his prominent erection as she lowered the zipper, he let out a hissing breath, his hands closing into fists.

"Della," he gasped as she removed his pants, leaving teasing licks up the length of his strong thigh.

"Shhh," she admonished, focused on her goal, enjoying this seduction. "This is what I want."

She took him into her mouth, experimenting to find what made him tense or arch closer, clench his hands or groan. He touched her gently, as if needing to keep touching her.

His breathing deepened, his muscles taut, but Della took her time. She set about discovering what he liked in great detail, memorizing every contour and every response. To her delight, some of her reading and research in such things ended up paying off, driving him nearly over the edge.

"Della, please, stop," he begged raggedly, reaching down to pull her up next to him. She met his eyes with a sense of wonder. *She* had put that look of raw desire and urgent need on his face, and it was like nothing she had ever experienced. She reached up to kiss him full on the lips, unable to stop touching him.

He accepted the kiss fervently as his hands were busy peeling the dress from her. She helped, starting to kick off her heels as well.

"No, those stay on," he said, breaking the kiss as he released her breasts from the scanty bra she wore.

"Wow," he said, tracing the edge of the transparent lace.

"It's new," she confessed, watching him caress her. She'd worried earlier if he would like it.

It was very clear that he approved, and then some,

though neither of them was in the mood to admire lingerie.

She felt sexy and wanton as he stepped back to take a long look at her standing there in her stockings and heels. Her self-consciousness was gone, completely. She knew how much he wanted her, and that knowledge made no room for doubts.

She turned to find her bag on a nearby seat, and took the protection she'd brought from inside, returning to him, not dropping her gaze from his as she covered him.

"I want *you*," she said, her limbs feeling molten. She liked this business of taking control, asking for what she wanted.

No more words were needed. He simply brought her up against him, their bodies and mouths meeting in an ecstatic reunion. Della was quivering from head to toe as he slowly lifted her knee to wrap her leg around the back of his.

He eased inside of her with such gentleness that tears threatened against the backs of her eyelids, but intense pleasure quickly chased them away. Already, their bodies knew each other so well. It was all so familiar, and yet everything was a new discovery, a new height she hadn't climbed before.

"You are the sweetest thing," he said against her lips, going in for another deep kiss. The embrace wiped any thoughts from her mind as she clung to him, letting him take over as she rode out the crest of a climax that had her sighing against him.

Gabe thrust faster as she came, his entire body hardening as he held her tight and buried his face in her neck, both of them beyond any coherent words. Her world was a blur of exquisite sensation as she hung on and she was momentarily shocked when he stopped, loosening his hold and stepping back from her for a moment.

His chest was heaving, glistening with sweat. She took him in, all hard muscle and jutting desire, feeling her knees go weak.

"Is something wrong?" she asked, unsure what made him stop.

"Honey, you're perfect. But come here, like this," he said, turning her so she could plant her hands on the edge of the stage next to them. He stood behind her, his hands coming around to her breasts as he filled her again. The resistance of the position made Della so hot she started moving against him, needing more.

"That's it, sweetheart," he encouraged as his big hands caressed her breasts and then dipped lower, catapulting her over the edge again.

He kept going, incredibly, telling her how gorgeous she was in great detail. How soft, how tight, how hot. He ran his hands over the backs of her thighs, admiring her shape and letting her know how beautiful she was until he was wordless and frantic, groaning. He soon brought her to yet one more knee-weakening orgasm, and let go along with her, his face buried at the side of her neck.

Tenderness welled inside of her at the way he held her, slowing his pace. She turned, wrapping her arms around him and holding him until they both caught their breath.

The star-filled space was quiet as they lowered down to the blanket. Della shivered a little, and Gabe grabbed his jacket, pulling it over her.

"No, I'm—" she objected, not wanting to ruin his coat, but he wrapped her in it anyway, keeping her snug against him.

They stayed that way for some while, and Della dozed off, waking up some time later to find Gabe asleep as well. She had no idea what time it was. They should probably leave before the cleaning staff came around to prepare for the next day, but she took several moments to look at Gabe's features in sleep, so relaxed and handsome. He was such a good man, she thought, but she was also sure he didn't believe that. She could tell, by the way that he touched her, and the things he said.

She could sense the tension inside of him, though. He did difficult things for his work, made tough calls, and it had a price. A lesser man wouldn't feel it the way Gabe did.

She reached out, running her hand over his chest, and then up to cup his jaw, stroking his cheek. His eyes opened, seeing her, smiling, and then wider, as he realized where they were.

"What time is it?" he asked, focusing on her with sudden sharpness.

"It's okay. I think we still have time to clear out before anyone shows up."

She leaned in to kiss him. "Thank you for tonight. This was amazing. I'll never forget it."

He seemed flustered by that, unsure what to say, which she found sweet. She was usually the one who was feeling awkward and unsure. Giving him a moment, she turned to grab her bag and phone, and checked the time.

"It's only a little after three, but we really should get going," she said with some measure of regret.

He nodded in agreement. They stood, quietly finding their clothes, dressing and picking up their belongings.

"Annie, the security guard you met, showed me which exit to use and the code for the lock."

"That's a lot of trust," he commented, walking beside her.

"We've been friends for a while, and I volunteer here on a regular basis. They change the codes every day," she said with a smile.

"I guess we'd better go before they change them and we have some explaining to do," he said with a smile.

Della liked to see Gabe smile, and she was honored that he seemed to do it a lot with her.

As they emerged out into the chilly early morning and walked toward the subway station, she turned to him.

"I want to see you again," she said in a soft tone. "I want as much of you as I can have, in the time you're here. But I know you have doubts, and work to do, so… if you want to see me, too, I'd love to hear from you. If not, I understand," she said, lifting up to kiss him one more time. "Thank you."

It was so difficult to turn around and walk away, not waiting for an answer. It was one of the hardest things she'd ever done.

Della wouldn't contact him again, not when she knew it could cause him problems or distract him from his work. He had to make that decision, and she would respect it.

She'd thought they could have an easy affair, but not

when there might be consequences. To his work, her heart. Perhaps it was best that this might be the last time she ever saw him.

The thought tugged at her as she stepped on the late night train, which was deserted, and sped toward her neighborhood. She chased the dread away, determined to live only in the moment, because the moment had been very good indeed.

5

GABE RAN DOWN the street by a small park, pushing his body to the limit, even though he'd gotten nearly no sleep again the night before. The day had been a complete loss, his concentration was shot. There had been a security breach at the lab—someone had made an attempt to steal the dummy information—but the connection had been untraceable, even by their experts.

And amid that, all he could think of was Della walking away from him three nights before. He'd decided not to contact her again, even though he wanted nothing more than to be with her, to lose himself in her softness, to escape the dark of his own reality by spending time with Della.

It wasn't fair. She didn't know who he was, or what he did. Not really, in spite of her empathy when they had spoken.

She had opened herself to him and he couldn't do the same. He was self-aware enough to know that what was between them was close to becoming about more than sex. So it was time to walk away, because that was what he was going to have to do anyway. It would hurt them both a lot more to do it later than sooner.

So he thought. It seemed the longer he was away from Della, the more he thought about her. Not good, especially now. Maybe a long, hard run would work off his frustration and allow him to clear his head and get some sleep.

He tried to shut out everything but work, to put her behind him, but the acute sensation of emptiness he'd experienced in her absence was unexpected. Gabe couldn't remember the last time he'd missed anyone.

He was probably missing the sex, but still. Turning around, he headed back toward the lab, where he could shower, change and get back to work. He had to find something soon, or they'd take him off the investigation.

Thoroughly spent, he took the elevator rather than the stairs, and walked into the locker rooms used by the science staff, where he had been given temporary accommodations. The showers were for daily decontamination, but they worked well enough to clean up. Back in his suit, he headed to the office, feeling a bit more focused.

Until he opened the door.

"Bart. What are you doing here?"

His boss raised an eyebrow, as if wondering why Gabe would be so surprised.

"There's new information, the kind I'd rather deliver personally."

Gabe frowned, closing the door. "Shoot."

"Look at these."

Bart handed him a folder. Most of the pictures were of a man, taken in various locations around the world.

His appearance was different in each shot, and Gabe assumed he took on different identities as well. That was par for the course.

"Who is it?"

"Cedric Derian," Bart answered. "He's an Armenian operative we've followed for a while." Bart indicated to him to keep paging through the report. "Derian's primarily an information broker for different governments, though he has been involved in some other aspects of trade, weapons, some human trafficking. He entered the US about a year ago, but we lost track of him shortly after that."

"About the time the vaccine project started up." Gabe's tone was grim.

Bart nodded. "He has to be the one after it—though we don't know for whom. We have to find him, who he's working with, and we have to stop him before he gets what he's after—which he is exceedingly good at."

Gabe nodded. "Any solid leads? I mean, he could be operating from anywhere."

"We're working on it. There was some chatter, but it's hard to trust at this point. Finding him takes precedence over everything else. We need to go back over all of the surveillance so far—all of it, the interviews, the reports—and dig deeper. He's connected to someone on the project, we just have to find out who and how. If we find his asset, they could lead us to him."

"Makes sense."

"Chances are, his asset is in danger, too. We can use that. Derian is not known for leaving loose ends. He wiped out his own team on his last job—he doesn't leave any connections behind, which is part of what makes it tough to track him. He makes sure no one is left behind who might lead to him."

Gabe frowned, studying the photos. Who was he posing as now, and where was he? Finding him in a city of eight million would be a good trick, unless they could get someone to talk.

And if he had to interview everyone he had already been investigating… This meant talking to Della again, too. Maybe.

"What?" Bart asked.

Gabe looked at him, and realized his very perceptive boss had read the change in his expression when he'd been thinking about Della.

Another reason he should stay away from her.

"Oh, nothing. I was just thinking about revisiting the interviews, where to start."

"You were thinking about someone in particular." It was a statement, not a question. Gabe had to come clean.

"There was a consultant, a mathematician who teaches at Columbia, who worked on the project early on. Dr. Della Clark. She did computational work, risk analysis, and she had no actual connection to the vaccine itself. I checked her out when I got here. I thought she might be a possibility, but she was clean. Probably not worth looking into again."

Bart leaned in, studying him closely. "How thoroughly did you check her out, if I might ask?"

Gabe took a breath. He and Bart had been friends, and had worked together, side by side, for a long time. Bart had moved up the ladder because he was better in management, and Gabe always preferred the field.

He'd been there when Janet died, and he'd always had his back. Bart knew Gabe well, and not just as an agent.

"I went through her files, computer records and emails, the usual. I also checked out her home, did the standard sweep. Nothing."

"And?"

Gabe dropped the file on the desk.

"And I slept with her. She was cute, and open to it. It was the easiest way to get inside her home."

"How many times?"

"What?"

"How many times did you sleep with her?"

"You mean in one night? Isn't that a little personal?"

Gabe's sarcastic deflection didn't work. Bart sighed.

"So I assume you've seen her more than once. You're involved?"

Gabe narrowed his gaze. "Are you asking as a friend or my boss?"

"Both. Is this something I should worry about in either case?"

Gabe shook his head. "No. I won't see her again. She's not likely to be involved beyond her initial work. She's very smart, but she's also…innocent."

"Not very, if she's sleeping with you," Bart said, huffing a laugh.

Gabe shot him a warning look, and realized that was what Bart was going for. His boss pinned him with a shark-like gaze.

"So you *are* involved. You didn't like me saying that. Listen, as your friend, knowing what you've been through, I'm happy for you, but this can't get in the way of this mission. I'll have someone else look deeper— you won't be objective."

Gabe bridled. "I've *already* checked her out, and I was thorough."

"Sounds like it."

"Bart—"

Bart put up a staying hand. "If you can't maintain objectivity in this investigation, Gabe, then I have to remove you from it—or at least from dealing with her. For your own safety as well as hers."

"It's not even worth bothering about, I'm telling you—"

Bart interrupted. "When you read the files, you'll see that Derian often uses academics—it's one of the few consistent things he's done. Dr. Clark could be more of a suspect than you think. That you are ruling her out so easily already makes me wonder if she hasn't snowed you, or if you're just letting the past affect your judgment. You haven't really been serious about anyone since Janet, and I can see in your face that you like this woman. Maybe more than like?"

Gabe sucked in his anger, cooled down. Bart was right. On every score.

"I'll admit, I don't want her to be involved. She's… a nice person. But I had a few doubts as well, and I can do my job. Frankly, if she is involved with Derian, and he is what you say he is, I *want* to be involved."

"So you can protect her."

"If necessary, yes. But she also trusts me. She's not going to trust someone else who just walks into her life so easily. She's not stupid."

Bart stared hard at him for several seconds, then nodded. "Fine. But you keep in touch with me, every step of the way. The main objective is not only finding Derian, but discovering who he's working for. We need to know who wants the vaccine, how much they know and who else might know. If it turns out that Dr. Clark needs to come in for interrogation, you inform me, and I'll do it."

Every one of Gabe's muscles tightened at the thought, but he knew he couldn't object as his gut did. He nodded stiffly instead. "Got it."

"You can do that?"

"I wouldn't like it, but I'll do my job."

Gabe meant that, and Bart knew he did. At the end of the day, he *would* do his job, even if he didn't like it. Most of all, he didn't let his friend see his resistance to letting anyone else investigate or interrogate Della, and he swallowed his own fear that she might be involved with Derian.

"I'll get into her house again, when she's not home— plant some surveillance, monitor her visitors through the local street cameras. And I'll bring Petroski back in, apply more pressure. Let her know she's in danger if she doesn't come clean."

"Wouldn't that be the approach to use with Dr. Clark as well? Or what about using her feelings for you? To make her tell you what she might know, if she thinks you are at risk in some way? Which you are, if she's working with Derian. Meaning this just became a lot more dangerous."

"I'll keep my guard up."

Bart frowned now. "You sure you're up for this, Gabe? After losing Janet, I wasn't positive you were even coming back to the job. That you could. If you care for this woman, this isn't exactly the way to build something, if you want to see her after this mission is over. If she's innocent."

"I don't want that." Gabe took a breath, feeling the tug of the lie in his chest. "She already knows that. Anyway, it's not the same thing, not by a long shot. Janet was my partner, and yes, we got involved emotionally. Losing her was…rough. But I've only known Della, Dr. Clark, for a week…less. I like her, but I'm not so far in that I can't let it go."

Bart stood, nodding. "Okay, then do it. If anything changes, I'll let you know. You do the same."

"I will."

Bart left and Gabe picked up the folder again, scrutinizing each picture of Cedric Derian, and then started planning his approach with Della and the other suspects.

He'd be lying if he didn't admit to the zing of anticipation at seeing her again, but he also feared for what he might find. With any luck, Della wasn't involved, as he originally suspected, and the only real danger either of them would be in was not being able to walk away again.

DELLA EMERGED FROM the subway station at 88th, soaking up the full bloom of the New York summer. Passing by tourists heading to the park and the natural history museum, she smiled at the children and admired the small gardens planted on stoops and in the alleys between the beautiful buildings in the area.

She was feeling as if she was in bloom as well, enjoying the sunny sky and the beauty around her after having worked all morning. She'd slept well and had put on a pretty summer dress—one delivered to her that morning, in a box, with simple instructions written in masculine handwriting. Heels, too.

Gabe.

Putting on the dress had been so intimate—especially as she thought about him taking it off when they met later that evening. He had only put a card with an address in the dress box, and nothing else.

It was exciting, and fun.

She liked how her shoes clicked along on the pavement. She had to learn to walk easily in them sometime, as she'd be wearing them at the wedding.

Her confidence was high, and that largely had to do with how one very handsome man made her feel about herself. Gabe believed she was beautiful, and sexy—and his desire for her was very persuasive. Della decided it was time she started thinking that about herself, too. If a man like Gabe wanted her so intensely, then why shouldn't she believe it?

She stopped by one stoop where fat, red tomatoes were drooping from their stems and the aroma of the fresh basil and peppers growing beside the concrete steps filled the air. An older man rose from his crouch behind a thick tomato bush, and she smiled at him through the vines.

"Hi, Vince. Your tomatoes are stunning, and passers-by can smell the basil before they get here. I wish I had your green thumb," she said, thinking about her sad little greenery on the terrace outside her bedroom.

"You're too kind, Della. You come by on your way home, I'll give you some for a sandwich. They are the best in the city," he said with a toothy grin.

She heard Vince, but was distracted by a man leaning on a car across the street. He looked familiar, like she had seen him somewhere before, but she couldn't place him. She shook her head at the notion, smiling at Vince.

"Maybe you can show me how to keep a plant alive one of these days," she said with a laugh, looking across the street again. The man was gone. "But until then, I'd love some of your tomatoes."

"How is your painting coming along?"

She sighed. "I haven't had much time for it. I'm on my way to dance lessons now, you know, for the wedding. It's been taking all of my extra time."

It was a small white lie. Della couldn't tell her friend that what had been taking a lot of her extra time was extremely hot sex with a man she met on a plane.

Vincent offered a raspy chuckle, his eyes narrowing under the rim of his wide gardening hat.

"There's a man, isn't there? You finally met someone on one of those dating websites?"

Della's jaw dropped in astonishment, and he laughed, waving her off.

"I have four daughters. I can tell when you have a man in your life. You look happy. I like the dress," he said with a wink. "It's reminiscent of Claude."

Della shook her head, but laughed, too. Vince was a sweet guy, a retired art professor who taught the watercolor class she took now and then. She looked down at the flowers on her dress. "They do look like a Monet, don't they? Like *The Iris Garden at Giverny*. That's probably why I liked it so much."

He nodded approvingly. It was one of his teaching tricks, to refer to artists by their first names, and see if his students could come up with the surname. But using great artists' first names also took the pressure off, made art seem more approachable, in a sense. Della appreciated that, since her painting was hardly expert, but she did it to expand her horizons and exercise her creative mind.

"The bright colors suit you. Will you be in the studio this month?"

She hesitated, and then shook her head with a tiny pinch of guilt. "Not until after the wedding, I'm afraid. But I promise, after that's over, I'll be a regular again."

He smiled and waved her on as they said goodbyes, and she rushed along the sidewalk to her class, making it right on time.

"Della, what a gorgeous dress!" her instructor, Ruth, exclaimed.

Other students in the class all turned to focus on her, and Della felt her cheeks warm, but she forced herself to meet the pointed attention head on. "Thank you, Ruth."

"You have to dance with Steven today, I think. You are tall enough in heels to dance with him."

Della swallowed, her nerves returning. Steven was Ruth's assistant, and very handsome. He was a professional dancer on Broadway who assisted Ruth part-time when he wasn't on stage himself. Several of her assistants were dancers she had taught over the years who came back to help with her classes, but Steven was the most good-looking.

Della always found him intimidating, certainly when she could barely avoid tripping over her own feet most of the time. He walked over to her and smiled engagingly, his grey eyes taking in her dress appreciatively.

"Good afternoon, Della. Ruth's right, that dress was

made for dancing," he said, and invited her to join him with a bow.

Della saw Stephanie, Steven's usual partner, glare at her from the other side of the studio. She looked away, remembering her newfound confidence, and smiled back at him. The music started and Ruth called for them to take their positions to continue practicing their swing dancing moves, which made Della bite back a groan. She hadn't been able to get the complicated, twisty movements right since she'd started learning them. Chloe, however, was having a swing band at the wedding, so Della had to learn the basics.

The music started and Steven led her through the first basic steps, which she did very well, even in her heels.

The first wrap-in, wrap-out went smoothly, and her confidence grew. Maybe she'd had the wrong partners before, because it seemed to be going much easier with Steven, who praised her as they went.

He also once, when they were in the sweetheart position, appeared to peek down the front of her dress. When she met his eyes with a surprised look, he winked at her, which made her misstep and nearly land on his toes with her heel.

Experienced in such things, Steven moved his foot deftly out of the way, but Della's good dancing streak was broken, and suddenly, she was flustered and missed the next few steps, no matter how Steven tried to get her back in the groove.

As the steps became more complicated she erred even more, and finally had to stop, frustrated, as the other dancers moved around them.

"I'm so sorry, I just… I'm never going to get this."

"It's my fault. I threw you off when I peeked down your dress," he admitted with a devilish smile. "Sorry about that. I should have been more discreet. But I didn't want to be."

Della blinked in response, unsure what to say as Steven led her over to the side of the room.

"I've always thought you were cute, but that dress just…wow. I don't suppose you'd want to go out sometime? Maybe have a private dance lesson? Or I could get us tickets to a show?"

Della's thoughts were scrambled and she didn't know what to say. Steven was actually asking her out. It was surreal. And she was seeing Gabe, but no…she was *sleeping* with Gabe. That was a whole different thing, right?

Was it okay to go on dates when she was sleeping with someone else? She had no idea how to calculate the angles of this unexpected development. Her life had never had so many interesting variables, but she had no experience solving this kind of a problem.

Thrown for the rest of the lesson, she left early and headed back to her office to work. It gave her time to think about what had happened with Steven. Regardless of the reality of her situation with Gabe, it felt wrong to date Steven—and maybe he meant more than date—while she was sleeping with Gabe.

What if she ended up having sex with both men? One at a time, of course, but still…talk about jumping in the deep end. She'd had no men in her life, and now she had too many. She hadn't even checked her dating profiles she'd been so busy, so who knew what was happening there? Maybe she should put her profile on temporary hold until she could catch up with what was happening in her real life.

She frowned as she looked out the window of the train, watching the walls and stops flash by, and wondered why she felt so guilty possibly accepting Steven's invitation, even though Gabe had made it clear he was just a temporary guy, and all they shared was sex. Taking a deep breath, she closed her eyes and tried to think logically. Reason and logic never let her down, and as she approached the issue that way, her answer appeared very quickly.

This was not a moral issue as much as one of timing. She simply was not ready to be with more than one man at a time, but Gabe was not likely to be around for more than a few weeks. A month at most, he'd said. So if she could make a date with Steven a few weeks down the line, perhaps for a show, that would solve the problem, right? Or she could even go to a show with him now, but no sex.

She squirmed a little in her seat, still feeling uncomfortable with seeing someone other than Gabe, at least at the moment, silly as it might seem. The train slowed down by her stop, and she stood, feeling like she had worked through the problem to some extent, anyway. For now, she was only seeing Gabe, and Steven was a nice possibility for the future.

Emerging up from the subway tunnel into the sun, she made the turn toward the university, where she could bury herself in the normality of work for a while, before it was time to go meet Gabe. As she walked to her building, a young man, probably a grad student, smiled at her and offered an appreciative glance.

This dress was a man magnet, she thought with a grin, knowing that probably wasn't what Gabe had intended. Would he be jealous if she saw someone else?

The idea thrilled her, but she shook it aside, knowing he probably wouldn't. They didn't have that kind of relationship—she frowned—or did they? She discovered, playing with the idea in her mind, that she didn't like the idea of Gabe with another woman.

That was even more reason for her to make plans with Steven, she decided as she took the elevator to the floor where her office was. She could easily fall for Gabe, and maybe she had already, just a little. If she was smart, she couldn't let it go any further.

But she didn't want to be smart. She'd been smart her entire life. She wanted to be stupidly, completely blind to consequences, odds, or risks for once, and she wanted to be that way with Gabe. Foolish, she reprimanded herself as she entered her office and settled down into work, hoping the stack of student research proposals and other projects would help her get these crazy ideas out of her head.

But it appeared nothing could erase Gabe from her senses. She worked, but kept noting the time, and how much longer until she went to meet him at their mystery location. Six o'clock. One more hour.

She grumbled at herself and her loss of perspective. It was one thing to want to be with him. It was another to pine and wait for him, staring at the clock.

Disgusted with herself and needing a break to stretch her legs, she rose and left her office, walking down the quiet, familiar hallways of her department. Only a few other people were around later in the afternoon, meeting with some students or working on papers, but she was here alone now.

Summer classes were in session, but the buildings were always more deserted this time of year, and she'd always valued that. She frequently worked until the wee hours, taking advantage of the quiet and aura of academia. Noting the names of her colleagues on the doors that lined the hall, minds greater than hers, she smiled, loving that she was counted among them. Most of them were older than her, and she couldn't call them friends, exactly, but she respected them, and she'd pushed herself to earn their respect.

No doubt they would not respect her if they knew what she had been up to recently. Certainly Dr. Aldi had never had wanton sex with a stranger he met on a plane.

But who knew? she thought with a smile, turning into the ladies' room.

Seconds later, she heard the door open again, and then close. Della didn't think much of it, but no footsteps crossed the floor to the stalls. Perhaps someone had thought it was the men's room.

Washing her hands and walking back out, she heard a noise behind her and turned to look, but no one was there.

The halls she had been reminiscing about suddenly seemed very lonely and crowded with echoes. She walked back toward her office, and was sure she heard footsteps somewhere behind her. As she glanced back, she did see someone turn the corner, and walked as fast as she could in her heels, her heart slamming in her chest.

College violence was still very much a reality. They

were in a large city, after all. She always reminded herself when she was on campus not to get too comfortable in her surroundings, ever, but doing so was inevitable. No one had ever had a problem in the department.

But she had a problem now. Footsteps echoed behind her as she reached her door, and pulled on it, finding it had locked behind her. A cry of fear and frustration escaped her lips, and she shoved a shaking hand into her bag, but she couldn't find her key.

Finally she did, as the heavier steps got even closer, just down around the corner now, and she slid the key into the lock, rushing into her office and locking the door behind her.

Moving to a far corner of the room, she stood out of sight, listening to the person approach her door, but… they didn't even stop, simply kept walking and then she heard the door at the end of the hall squeak open—the heavy metal door that led to the stairwell.

She let go of a breath she felt like she had been holding ever since coming into the room, and looked at her hands. They were shaking. So were her legs, and she walked unsteadily to her chair, and sank into it, dropping her head into her hands.

Then her overactive imagination poked at her, wondering if the person had actually left the floor, or were they out in the hall, lying in wait?

All the while chastising herself for being ridiculous, she walked to her door, steeling herself to open it—but she also brought the small can of pepper spray she kept in her purse.

Peeking outside, she saw nothing, and opened the door wider.

Empty.

Her heartbeat slowed slightly, but she was too afraid to venture out of her office, just in case. Feeling foolish, she called security and asked them to walk her down from her office, even if it wasn't dark yet.

"Is there a problem, Professor?" the guard asked, with a concerned voice.

"I thought someone was outside my office earlier, but they left. It just spooked me, I guess. Thank you for coming up."

"No problem. Better safe than sorry," he agreed and they chatted generally as they walked back down to the quad.

Della felt even more ridiculous when they emerged out into the filtered sun of the early summer evening.

"Thank you," she said. "I appreciate the escort, but I'm fine from here."

He tipped his hat and walked away, and Della strolled the sidewalk of the quad, taking in the beautiful buildings of the institution that she loved like a second home. It was awful to feel unsafe here, and she didn't want that feeling to linger, especially when it was just a product of her own paranoia.

Looking at her phone, she saw the time and picked up her step. She'd need to make the train soon in order to meet Gabe at the appointed time, having wasted so much of it hiding in her office.

The thought of being with him moved her along faster, not just because she wanted to see him, but because the idea of being with him made her feel safe. And that was something she very much needed right now. No matter how she tried to talk herself into being rational, she caught herself looking over her shoulder, still feeling as if someone might be following her.

She didn't shake the feeling until she was on the train speeding toward downtown. Speeding toward Gabe.

6

GABE SAW DELLA ARRIVE, the dress he sent her standing out in the dim evening light as she walked by the large windows at the front of the bar, and in the door. He rose to greet her at the door with a light kiss, taking her in.

"You look gorgeous."

"Thank you. This was very generous. I love the dress. It was a very sweet thing to do," she said with a slight smile, though her eyes looked strained and her hair was slightly mussed.

"Is everything okay?" he asked, looking more closely.

She hesitated before responding, which gave him his answer, even though a second later she nodded with a too-bright smile and told him she was fine.

Gabe let it go for the moment, and took her hand, leading her back to their table.

"This isn't quite as creative as your invitation to the museum, but I thought it would be nice to go on a date," he said, taking a sip of his drink. "You know, dinner, drinks, maybe some dancing. The kind of night out you deserve, Della."

He was no lightweight, but he'd had two drinks before this and the third Scotch was starting to ease the guilt eating away at him. He was only here to insinuate himself into her life, to get closer, to see if he'd been wrong about her.

"Dancing? Oh, you don't want to go there," she said with a rueful shake of her head as a waitress delivered her drink and took their orders.

"Why not?"

"More maid-of-honor duty. Namely, dancing lessons, or as they are otherwise known, the seventh level of hell."

He chuckled. "It can't be that bad."

"Thanks, but you should have seen me in these heels in my dance class today—total geek. Stepped on my partner's feet, several times."

"This is for the wedding? Learning to dance?"

"Uh-huh. I will have to at least do the required dances, and I have never danced at all, with anyone, outside this class. It's nerve-wracking."

"No proms? School dances?"

"I was too young to attend. You know, math prodigy and all that, I was in grad school before most of my peers were out of high school, so that really messed up my social life. As in, I didn't have one. Not after the ninth grade. Before that was more or less normal."

"Really? I knew you were smart, I didn't know you were a child genius."

She rolled her eyes back, laughing. "Only with numbers. For everything else I only had a normal ability, and when it came to social things, I was way below average."

He reached out, touching her cheek. She looked

ethereal in the soft light of the bar, which was decked out in dark woods, cozy corners, like the one they sat in, and leather chairs. Gabe often came here alone when he was in the city, but it seemed right somehow to share it with Della.

"There's nothing below average about you."

She shrugged. "I'm just not used to it, even now."

"That must have been very difficult. To miss out on so much."

Her lips fell into that sad frown he observed from time to time. He had a feeling Della had been lonely for a good part of her life, and knowing that triggered an ache in his chest. Especially since she deserved better than what he was offering her, that was for sure. Maybe Bart was right—maybe he was too involved, because he couldn't see Della being a part of this mess, unless it was as an unknowing victim. There was just no way—he started to think this entire evening was a mistake, except that he enjoyed being with her so much.

"Well, like I mentioned, I don't date a lot. And I certainly never had two sexy men interested in me before."

That definitely caught his attention.

"Um, two?" he asked, drawing back just a bit.

She closed her eyes in chagrin. "Sorry, I didn't mean to blurt that out—it was so thoughtless. I think this drink is getting to me. I didn't get lunch, and then—"

She paused again, clamping her lips shut as if she was about to let yet another slip escape.

Gabe's senses sharpened, and he leaned in, a classic maneuver to invite someone to confide. To trust. He couldn't turn off who he was, what he did, even now. Not really.

"Tell me what's going on, Della. I could see when

you came in that something was bothering you—does it have to do with this other guy?"

His muscles tensed, and he realized he would not react well to someone threatening Della.

He could stay objective, right.

Her shoulders fell in defeat, but her voice was steady. "No, it's two different things. I had a dance lesson today, and one of the dance instructors came on to me, asked me out. It was a huge surprise. Then, I was at work, and I thought someone was following me."

"Following you?"

"Yes. I was in the ladies' room, and I thought someone was following me back to my office, but they weren't. I was just being jumpy. It was later in the day, and I was there alone. Really, there's nothing to be worried about." She smiled weakly. "I think this whiskey is some kind of truth serum."

"Why do you think it was a mistake?"

"They kept walking and left the building, never even stopping at my door. I did get a campus security guy to walk me down to the quad, even though I felt like a moron afterward."

"No, you definitely shouldn't feel that way. Following your instincts, listening to your fear, is how people stay alive."

"It's not that I don't agree with that, in principle, but it was very likely this was just my imagination working overtime."

Gabe let it rest since their dinners had arrived, but as he cut into his steak, he decided to prod a bit more.

"So this dance instructor, you've known him for a while?"

"Well, I only started lessons three months ago, so

only since then, and usually he works with other, better dancers, but for whatever reason, Ruth stuck him with me, today."

"Ruth?"

"Ruth Avakian, the owner of the school. She was a famous ballerina once, and now she teaches ballet, but also regular dancing to people like me," Della said with a smile. "I needed all the help I could get, so I was lucky to get into her class on such short notice. Steven is her assistant."

Gabe's mind was ticking through the possibilities, and the time line of events. That there had been a move on the vaccine formula, and now two men—unless Della's follower was the dance instructor—suddenly had approached her in two days. He didn't know exactly what to make of it, but by Della's own admission, this wasn't commonplace in her life. And he knew Ruth Avakian—who didn't? She was famous for her years of dance, and she was also Armenian by birth, though she had danced in the New York City ballet and lived here through adulthood.

A contact for Armenian spies? Could she have infiltrated through the ballet? Could she be helping Cedric Derian, or at least know of his whereabouts? Was this dance instructor, Steven, really Cedric?

If so, then Steven's sudden interest in Della wasn't good.

"Oh, this steak is delectable," she purred as she took a bite, and all of Gabe's rational thought went out the window, watching the juicy bit of meat disappear between lush lips, her eyes closing as she enjoyed it.

He shifted in his seat, looking away again, to his own meal, trying to refocus. He was in too deep, wanting to make sure that Della was safe, and to do whatever it took to keep her that way, but he was losing his objectivity. He should call Bart back, but that wasn't going to happen. His friend would take him off the case immediately.

"It is good," he agreed lamely, eating his perfectly cooked steak, which he barely tasted as he fought the war of concern, suspicion and desire waging inside of him.

There was more than a decent chance that Della wasn't being paranoid about someone following her.

"Anyway, it was a sort of crazy day, that's for sure," she said with a satisfied sigh as she took a sip of her drink.

"As a man who thinks you are very attractive, I find it hard to believe other men don't walk over each other trying to get to you," he said. "You, sweetheart, are naturally sexy. Take my word for it. Every man at the bar noticed you when you walked in. So are you going to see this guy…what's his name?"

Her blush deepened, and he was very happy when she shook her head.

"No, well, not while you and I are, um, seeing each other, but maybe for the wedding, I don't know…" she said, clearly uncomfortable.

"I'm sorry for prying. I know it's none of my business," he said, and thought he saw some disappointment dull the warmth in her eyes.

"It's okay. I don't mind at all," she said, swallowing hard and dropping her gaze as she fiddled with her food, awkwardness settling between them.

She didn't mind because she hoped he would be jealous, he realized. Was that the point? Was there even a mysterious dance instructor, or was this Della's attempt to see if he had feelings for her?

And did he?

Yes. That meant it would be much easier for him to get closer, deeper, into her life. Because she wanted him there.

"I stuck my foot in it, didn't I? And after you went through all this trouble for such a nice date."

"Not at all," he quickly reassured her. "Truthfully, it's my fault. I shouldn't have pushed, but I guess even though we only agreed on a temporary relationship, I still don't like the idea of you with another man."

That was the absolute truth, and he saw her eyes widen, her color deepen. Her eyes warmed again—she was pleased.

"Oh, well, then," she said a little breathlessly, and turned her attention to the sound of the band starting up at the back of the room.

As they started playing a slow jazz number, Gabe stood.

"Let's dance, Della."

She looked apprehensive, but he held out his hand, and she took it. A few other couples also filled the dance floor.

"I'm not exactly Baryshnikov, either. Let's just dance. You don't have to worry."

She laughed softly. "You do—about your toes," she joked nervously.

But Gabe didn't want her to be nervous with him. About anything. He wanted her to let go and be herself, and that was more important than he would have imagined. That she trusted him enough for that in spite of their situation. That she would trust him enough to tell him anything, or to let him into her life as deeply as he needed to be to keep her safe.

He brought her up against him, and put his lips by her ear, inhaling the scent of her hair.

"Just move with me, Della. Like when we're making love," he said as she shivered against him.

Gabe hadn't danced in a long time. Years. He'd forgotten how much he enjoyed it, actually, as they found their rhythm together. Or maybe it was because he was dancing with Della. She was stiff at first, and she did almost step on his toe in those heels.

"Oh, sorry, I—" She started to pull away, and he pulled her right back in.

"The song's not over, Della," he said.

She had such a look of concentration on her face, like she was solving some terribly difficult problem. He understood, in a way, how she might approach unfamiliar things with her brain instead of her instincts, since that was what she was used to.

So he brought her attention back to her body by running his hands over her backside, squeezing lightly as he pressed her close, and heard her catch her breath.

Then he dropped light, teasing kisses along the line of her neck to her jaw, and over to her lips, until that furrow between her eyes was smooth, and her face had relaxed.

"That's it," he said softly, turning her around slowly in spite of the lively beat, bringing her back against his front, their arms wrapped around each other. Then he unwrapped her just as slowly, turning her under the bridge of his arm and bringing her back to face him.

"Hey, that's the wrap-in, wrap—"

"Don't name it, sweetheart. Feel it. Have fun with it."

She smiled when he turned her again, and then she did a quick kick step, picking up the rhythm, and by the end of the song, they were both dancing an easy swing and laughing.

Gabe hadn't felt this good in a long time. They danced through two more songs, one more slow and sexy, and then a faster dance that made their pulses race. But as they moved, and all of her curves fit so nicely against him, Gabe's mind wasn't so much on dancing.

"Did you want dessert?" he asked.

"Oh, no, I'm stuffed. But maybe we could take a walk? It's a gorgeous night. Are you familiar with the city?"

"Somewhat, but I'm usually working, not here for enjoyment."

"Then let me show you some of the sights."

He couldn't think of anything nicer than walking under the brilliant city lights with this woman, and took her hand.

"Sounds perfect," he said, lifting her fingers to his mouth for a moment and anticipating what the night ahead held in store.

DELLA WAS HAVING what she was certain would be one of the most romantic evenings of her life, certainly of her life so far. She'd worried that she had almost ruined everything when she made the slip about Steven—stupid whiskey lowering her inhibitions—but then when Gabe had admitted he was a bit jealous, her heart had nearly swelled out of her chest.

That she knew of, it was the first time any man had ever been jealous with regard to her. It was...an odd feeling, both powerful and a bit frightening, to see that possession cross his face, the dangerous glint in his eyes.

And arousing. Definitely that.

Walking along with a handsome man, holding hands as they strolled the smaller streets of downtown and the Lower West Side, was like something from one of the New York City movies she watched over and over again.

The evening was still warm and humid, but there was a breeze that filtered through, making their stroll a pleasant one. They stopped by a small park and sat on a bench, enjoying the cooler evening with others who were doing the same outside their small apartments. As they sat, Gabe rubbed his thumb on the nape of her neck, which made her feel much warmer.

A short time later, they walked closer to the center of the city and ducked into the Empire State Building, which Gabe said he'd never visited. Della was thrilled to be able to be the tour guide, showing him some of her favorite neighborhoods and sights. As they rode the elevator up to the observation deck, a ripple of excitement ran through her.

"I never get tired of the view here. I love this city, and the deck shouldn't be too crowded this time of night."

"I can't wait," he said, pulling her up close against him and nuzzling her ear.

She turned into him, ignoring the few other people in the car who were not paying attention anyway, and pressed her lips to his throat at the opening of his shirt.

Della watched the pulse there pick up, and smiled. She was feeling bold, encouraged by his openness, and he didn't seem to mind one bit. Then the doors behind her opened up, and she stepped back, her smile widening.

"Here we go!" she said, taking his hand and pulling him out through the small shop and onto the deck.

The city sprawled out before them. Together, they went to the least crowded spot on the deck, which wasn't very busy anyway. It was like they had the entire place and the entire city, to themselves.

They stood side by side as she pointed out various features of the city, and one of her favorites, the water towers that supplied water to so many of the buildings.

She felt closer to Gabe after his revelation—being jealous meant he had to have some feelings for her, right?—and that changed everything, as did his willingness to walk along with her through the city. He wasn't only going along with her for sex. He seemed to really enjoy spending time with her. Della supposed it was true, that women really did need an emotional connection to a man they were sleeping with, even when it was only a fling.

"It's really beautiful. I've always known it was, but I never really took the time to look," he said, staring out over the lights and the city landscape. Then he looked down at her. "Thank you," he said.

Something about the expression on his face, and his tone, touched her. As if he hadn't experienced enough of what was beautiful in life, and had perhaps forgotten that it was there.

"My place is about five miles in that direction," she said, pointing.

He walked her back into the corner of the metal

fencing, and lowered for a kiss that quickly became hot and left her wanting more when he pulled away.

"Time to go, then?" he asked, sounding somewhat raspy himself.

"Absolutely."

The tone of his voice and heat in his gaze made every nerve ending in her body tingle. And Della knew that was only the beginning.

They made their way back down to the ground floor, and as they walked out onto the sidewalk, nearly collided with a couple heading inside.

"Della! What are you doing down here?"

Della refocused, and then smiled, accepting the hugs from Chloe and Justin as they stood on the walk.

"We were just out for a stroll."

"And this is?" Chloe said, sliding her gaze and a beaming smile at Gabe.

"Chloe Brown, this is Gabe Ross. Gabe, this is my friend Chloe, and her fiancé, Justin Nelson."

Gabe stepped in, offering a smile in return and shaking hands with her friends. Della watched his expression change, becoming less open, though still pleasant. Generic. The heat, passion and light that had been there only seconds before completely disappeared, as if he had donned a mask.

It was fascinating and disconcerting all at once, to see him draw back in so effectively. It also made her realize how open he had been with her.

"You should come out for coffee with us. The night is young," Chloe exclaimed with her classic exuberance. "We won't take no for an answer."

"But weren't you going up?"

Chloe waved her off. "We were getting some air

and thought we'd go up, but you know we've seen it a million times. I'd rather visit with you."

Della shared a helpless look with Gabe and sighed. Chloe was a force of nature.

"I suppose an iced coffee would be nice," she said, caving to her friend's demands.

Gabe only smiled briefly, and walked a short distance to a small Italian coffee shop where they all squeezed into a small booth, ordering their drinks.

"So, Gabe, Della mentioned you were with Homeland Security. That has to be an exciting job," Chloe said.

Della could detect the slight stiffening in Gabe's posture since they were sitting so close together in the booth. In fact, their hips and thighs were pressed tight against each other and Della found it distracting in the most lovely way.

Impulsively, she slipped her foot out of her sandal and touched it to his ankle, nudging her foot up under the cuff of his slacks. That would help him relax a bit, she thought mischievously. He jumped slightly at the contact, and then cleared his throat before responding to Chloe.

"That's right, but it's not very exciting, really. I'm involved mostly with logistics. It's a lot of computer time, sitting at a desk. Lots of reports and meetings. None of the exciting stuff," he lied as naturally as he smiled.

Della knew why he had to do that, but she also found it disconcerting. She was regretting very much telling Chloe anything about Gabe.

She cast him a concerned glance, but the smile he offered her was sincere. He draped his arm over the back of the narrow booth, sliding his fingers under her hair to rest on the nape of her neck. The weight of his hand there made her shiver with anticipation. It felt possessive and protective all at the same time.

"Isn't that always the way?" Chloe said, not seeming to notice the subtle seduction going on right across the table. "I worked as a model for a while in college, and everyone thought that was all glamour, but it wasn't. Wearing layers of cosmetics, your hair so full of product that your head itches, but you can't touch it, all while standing around for hours in front of hot cameras in uncomfortable shoes. I didn't last a year," she said with a shake of her head.

"What did you end up doing?" Gabe asked as he lowered his arm again, setting it in his lap. Della missed the contact, and took a sip of her coffee, sliding him a look and licking her lips.

His eyes flashed with something hot, and she looked down, smiling to herself.

This was fun.

"I work in the math and science department at Columbia, which is where Della and I met. I'm a full-time research assistant. I help professors like Della with their scholarly work, do some of the grunt work while they teach and write, that kind of thing."

"She makes it sound like nothing, but we'd be lost without her," Della said warmly, offering her friend a smile. "And she has her doctorate in research methodology, so she does a lot more than the grunt work."

Justin had been quiet to this point, but that wasn't unusual. Della liked him, but he was very reserved, typically observing more than he participated. Maybe that was why he and Chloe matched so well; they were completely opposite. "I'm a self-employed IT analyst," he offered, breaking into the conversation. "I'm also a gun collector. What kind of weapon do you normally use on the job? I read that the P226 is standard, but do you get a choice of weapon?" Justin asked.

Gabe shrugged. "I don't carry for my job, but most guys I know are issued SIGs. They like them. A lot have their own personal weapon, of course. How many guns do you own?"

Justin smiled. "Eighty-five, most of them antiques. All legal, don't worry."

Gabe laughed. "Don't worry, that's not my wheel-house, and I'm off-duty."

Della caught a breath as his hand slipped from the table to her thigh and slid upward, no doubt a signal for them to say their goodbyes. The feel of his touch, moving ever closer to the crease of her hip, was all the inducement she needed.

"This is great, guys, but we need to get going. It was fun bumping into you."

"We hope we'll see you again, Gabe. There are several wedding events in the next few weeks and consider yourself welcome as Della's plus-one, if you like," Chloe said.

Della wanted to kick her friend in the shin, and sent her a glare.

"Thank you, that's very generous of you," Gabe said. "Maybe I will, if Della wants my company." He looked over at Della, who was unable to hide her surprise.

They slid out of the booth and left the coffee shop, and Gabe tried to grab a few taxis, but they were off-duty or already taken.

"It was nice of you to say that, but I know you were

just being polite," she said reasonably, squeezing his hand reassuringly so he had an "out."

"It depends on the case I'm working, and if I'll be around, but if I am, I think it might be fun. I haven't been to a wedding in quite some time. And we'd have another chance to dance," he said, smiling at her.

"That would be nice. I would definitely enjoy your company, no doubt about that."

"Likewise."

"Let's walk up a few blocks, and we might have more luck, or we can just take the subway," Della said.

"I don't know if I can keep my hands off of you that long."

The way he said it, so serious, so…intense, made her tingle from head to toe.

"Me, either."

She stopped, looking at the hotel they stood in front of, and then at him with the question in her eyes. He nodded.

Ten minutes later, Gabe was pressing her up against the wall of a hotel elevator, showing her just how urgent his need was. His kiss crushed her lips and she devoured him back. His hands were everywhere, and he muttered something about a security camera, but she didn't care.

Neither did he, as he lowered his head to suck the tip of her breast into his mouth right through the fabric of her dress, making her cry out. Her hands traveled down over his chest to cover the hard evidence of how turned on he was, and when the bell finally rang and the doors opened, they couldn't get out and down to their room fast enough.

Della giggled like a girl, though this was certainly

not something she'd ever done when she was young. She hadn't gone to proms or parties, or to hotels with her date afterwards, as so many other girls did.

And she didn't care, because if she had to miss all of that in order to experience all of this with Gabe, then it was worth it.

He had the key, and they ducked inside the room—a suite, since there hadn't been a regular room left. Gabe hit the light by the door and locked it behind them, then pulled her into another kiss.

Della sighed against his mouth as he eagerly slipped off his jacket and she tugged at his tie while she kicked off her shoes.

She tripped over him as he kicked off his as well, and he caught her, which led to several more minutes of very arousing kisses. If all he wanted to do was kiss all night, she'd be up for it, she thought, though he definitely had other things in mind.

7

THE SIMPLE TOUCH of her lips to his skin zipped through him like a lightning bolt, and he pulled her closer, wanting more. He found her lips, explored and teased, walking her backward into the room as they kissed.

This time, he took it slower. Della liked to be kissed, and he was happy to accommodate, tasting her with long, deep, drugging kisses that made him lose track of everything as well.

Her hands drifted over him, her fingers closing on the fabric of his shirt when she gasped and held on as he dragged his lips from her mouth down the line of her jaw to her throat. And then down the deep scoop of the dress, above her breasts.

He lingered there for a while, liking the feel of her heartbeat against his lips and his jaw, before he rose to take possession of her mouth again.

She was so sweet and curvy, he thought, absently sliding his hands down over her rear so he could press her into his erection. He liked the noise she made when he did that, so he pressed in more, and enjoyed it a second time.

"Della, honey, turn around," he whispered in her ear.

She turned, his hands on her shoulders, until her back was to his front. Sliding his hands around, he covered both of her breasts, enjoying their sensual weight, and how her nipples pressed through the fabric as if eager for his touch.

Della moaned as he fingered them, making them even harder, and him, too. Especially when she cleverly insinuated a hand behind her, closing her fingers around his shaft.

It was as close as he'd ever been to coming too soon, since he'd been a much younger man.

Taking his hands away from her breasts, he kissed her nape as he found the zipper of her dress again. The zipper slid down easily, and he pushed one side of the dress from her shoulder, revealing a pretty bra strap. Black satin lined a strip of transparent gauzy stuff; that alone made his imagination do acrobatics wondering what the rest would look like. Was it all see-through? All black?

His fingers trembled slightly as he pushed the fabric away from her other shoulder and then the rest of the way down. The dress fit loosely and didn't need more help than that to fall to her feet, showing him everything.

"Sweet," he breathed, falling to his knees and shaping his hands up the backs of her thighs and over the smooth, silky, see-through material with satin edging. "Gorgeous."

He turned her around, slowly, and she gazed at him with those beautiful curls surrounding her face, her eyes uncertain, lips parted, cheeks flushed. She was so damned sexy he was about to lose it.

"You are incredible. You don't need to wear things like this to be flat-out beautiful, but it sure is a treat."

His gaze drifted from the patch of curls nested under the sheer fabric, to her breasts, which seemed even more perfect, framed with the strips of black satin.

Talk about eye candy, this was more of a feast. He couldn't stop looking at her. Looking led to touching, which quickly made him want to taste.

Hooking his thumbs under the band of those lovely, tempting panties, he pulled them down her smooth thighs, exposing what he wanted to see. She stepped out of them and sighed when he slipped his hands in between her knees, widening her stance.

"You're walking temptation, Della Clark," he said, dragging his tongue up the inside of her thigh, loving everything about being so close to her. Her scent, her taste and how she responded with sighs and moans as he explored further, kissing her more intimately.

As he circled his tongue around the sensitive flesh of her sex, he listened, seeing what made her moan, what made her cry out or seek more of what he was offering. He hadn't had such fun learning a woman's body in a long time. Her knees sank slightly as he pushed her toward the edge of bliss. Then he stopped.

"Maybe we should find the bed," he suggested, his voice rough with desire as he glanced up at her.

She was a vision, so aroused, full and soft and quivering. He stood and swept her up in his arms before she could respond, carrying her to the bed. She laughed, clinging to him and clearly having fun. It was a joyful sound that kicked off his own smile as he laid her down, watching her as he shucked his clothes quickly.

He leaned in with a hand braced on either side of

her shoulders, taking her in again, committing her, and this moment, to memory.

"Don't ever doubt yourself, Della. You're insanely beautiful," he said against her lips, before finding his way down her body again, settling in between her thighs and using every trick he knew to make her insane with need.

"Gabe, please, please," she begged breathlessly.

He was on the edge as well, her arousal feeding his, so he granted her request. When she came, she arched from the bed, crying his name, and Gabe was dizzy from knowing he'd done that for her.

He wanted to do more.

Raising up over her, he settled down, covering her, finding her mouth for a kiss. She offered herself to him like a ripe peach, and the furious need that surged through him made him harden the kiss, his cock thrusting against the softness of her belly.

Panting, he pulled away before he did something really stupid and forgot to protect both of them.

"Give me a second," he said, leaving her to find one of the condoms he'd brought with him.

He met her eyes as she watched him roll it on, and saw that made her breath catch. He paused, his gaze never leaving hers as he stroked his hand along his length. Her nipples peaked in response, and he enjoyed that, too, so he fought for self-control, letting her watch a little more before he couldn't risk finishing before he intended. Right now, he wanted to be as deep inside Della as he could get. They could make time for the other later.

The word stuttered in his mind as he returned to the bed. Would there be a later? In the immediate sense, yes, but he had to be careful about thinking in the future tense.

It didn't take long before he gasped as she closed around him, tight and hot, making him clench his jaw in an effort to hold on. He'd never wanted to let go so badly, but he also never wanted it to end. Being inside her like this was the most amazing thing he'd ever felt, and he wanted to make it last as long as possible.

But Della had other ideas, apparently. With a scorchingly sexy look, she drew him down flush against her, into her arms, her legs locking over the backs of his thighs. Gabe wrapped his arms around her instantly.

She kissed him, gently at first, but as the kiss deepened and became more carnal, she started to move, rotating her hips in a rhythm that triggered a groan from deep inside him. The slight tingling at the base of his spine, the heat that raced through his blood and straight to his cock, told him he was ready.

When Della claimed his mouth as her body pulsed around his, Gabe couldn't hold on any longer. The resulting climax seemed to go on forever. He was captivated by Della's kiss, by her softness and warmth. For a few wonderful minutes, his world was only made of Della and the pleasure they shared.

But it did. The pleasure ebbed, and he fell to her side, letting her breathe, and caught his own breath as well. He left her only to dispose of the condom, then returned to settle beside her.

"That was…" Della began.

"Mind-blowing," he said, finishing her thought.

She looked at him with a big grin. "I was about to use that exact word."

She still had the bra on, and he reached out, touched

the tip of her breast, and she bit her lip as her body responded.

"I love that bra. But I think we'll take it off soon."

"I'm glad you like it. Really," she said, so softly it landed somewhere in his chest, making him warm in a different way. "It's new. Chloe talked me into buying some new things when we were shopping for bridesmaid's dresses."

"I can't wait to see you in yours. Or is it something awful, like you see in YouTube videos? Big pink puffs of some awful fabric or something?" he asked, grinning.

She laughed. "No, it's a beautiful dress. I can't wait to wear it, actually. Even more so if you can be there, too."

Gabe resolved that as long as nothing went terribly wrong, whether the current case was closed or not, he was going to accompany her to these wedding events. It was the least he could do, given the circumstances.

He liked Della. He didn't only like having sex with her, he liked *her*. She was sweet and real, with no pretense or games. He had had far too much of the latter in his life. So much so that he couldn't tell lies from the truth anymore, it seemed.

The problem was that he was still lying to her, and he had no choice but to continue to do that. The realization made him lay back and stare at the ceiling as he pondered what the hell he was doing.

He was still leaving New York as soon as he finished this job, and then Gabe Ross would cease to exist. She wouldn't be able to find him even if she tried. Once upon a time, that reality would have offered him the escape he always kept handy. Now it left a strange, nagging feeling in his chest.

As much as he might have a soft spot for her, he was still using her for sex, and there couldn't ever be much more to it than that. She wanted that, too, obviously. But she wasn't experienced enough to be that easy about the intimacy.

"What are you thinking about?" she asked, reaching out to touch his chest, running her fingers over his skin.

"You," he answered honestly. He'd give her honesty where he could, as much as he could.

"Hmmm. Are you thinking about this bra again?"

She preened in a seductive pose on the bed, and he grinned.

"I am now."

"Good."

She lifted up to her knees, throwing a leg over his thighs and straddling him. She reached behind and undid the clasp on the bra, letting her pretty breasts free.

"What are you thinking about now?" she asked, teasing.

"Come here and I'll show you," he teased back, pulling her down for a kiss and groaning at the lovely press of her soft breasts against his chest.

She sighed into his kiss, and the heat built again as he hardened.

There would be a moment where he'd have to walk away from Della Clark, he knew that, and maybe it would be sooner than later. But as she cuddled against him, heat consumed him again as he reached for another condom, and he knew that moment wasn't going to happen tonight.

TWO DAYS AFTER her date with Gabe, Della emerged from a building in midtown, near the Garment District, feeling dazed. She'd been to four male strip clubs so far that evening, and she was feeling rather overwhelmed with images of glistening pectorals and muscled thighs. Definitely a case of too much of a good thing.

She wished she had someone who was more experienced in planning a bachelorette party to come with her, but she was Chloe's maid of honor, and no one else had been available that evening. Unfortunately, she'd probably waited too long as it was to make any plans.

Gabe had emailed her an invitation to meet, but she couldn't really tell him what she was up to that evening, but had made a general excuse, hoping he hadn't felt put off. Still, for all the exposed male flesh she'd seen in the last three hours, not one single man on the stage had compared to Gabe. Thinking about him standing over her, naked by the bed, made her shiver as she walked down the street toward her next and final club for the evening.

She wished she had accepted his invitation, but the bachelorette party was in a week and a half, and she had put this off as long as she could. Maybe she'd call Gabe and see if he wanted to meet for breakfast.

Standing in front of the door to the club she'd been heading toward, she balked. Maybe she just wasn't up to one more show, but the strip-club option for the party felt like a cliché. Still, Chloe would enjoy something adventurous, not just a nice dinner with some dirty jokes or prank gifts.

Della truly was at a loss.

Deciding to pass on the last strip club, she kept walking, enjoying the cool air of the evening, and missing Gabe. Then, as she stopped at a corner, waiting to cross, she saw a flyer with bright colors announcing a "sensual cooking" class—a feast for all of the senses.

Pausing, she read more, and saw there was a class happening that evening, starting in an hour. They also did parties! Maybe this was her break—something original *and* sexy. She could have a sensual cooking party for Chloe.

Wasn't it better to send her friend into married life celebrating her sensual future with her husband-to-be, instead of acting like this was her last chance to gawk at a bunch of naked men on a stage?

The more Della thought about it, the more she liked it, and she pulled down the flyer, heading toward the address stated on the front, which wasn't too far away, near the culinary school.

On the way, she paused, the hairs on the back of her neck suddenly standing up. She didn't know why, but she now felt as if she was being followed.

The incident from her office had almost been forgotten, but now came back in a blinding rush. She turned, peering circumspectly around her, but didn't see anything or anyone in particular. It had to be her imagination, but still…

She turned and headed down the street again, holding her bag closer and staying amid the throng of evening walkers. She was safe here, in the middle of the busy street, right?

She was relieved when she found the address, and walked in, spotting a group of people lined up at a desk. It appeared to be the registration line for the class. Joining in, she finally got to the desk, and took out her credit card to pay, when the young woman sitting there shook her head.

"We do have one free table left, but this is a couples' class, I'm afraid." The young woman looked at her apologetically, and perhaps with a tiny edge of judgment.

Della felt the warmth invade her cheeks as the people behind her must have heard, but she pulled herself up straight and smiled. "I am part of a couple. My... partner, is at work, and will join me shortly. I'll pay for us both. I'd also like information on booking parties here, a bachelorette party in particular."

"That's terrific—we've had some very good parties, here," the woman said, handing her another flyer. "Just be aware, if your partner tonight doesn't make it, you'll have to forfeit the class without a refund, though you can rebook for another night."

"That's fine."

As soon as she was by the desk, she called Gabe, who answered on the second ring.

"Della, what's up? I thought you were busy tonight."

"I was. I am... I just... I need you."

"Well, that's nice to hear," he said, lowering his voice to a more intimate level, which made her smile.

"Not that way... I mean, I do—need you that way—but not at the moment, though sort of—"

"Della, what's going on?"

"I'm sorry, I couldn't meet you because I had to do some bachelorette party research, and I think I've found a perfect alternative, but I need a partner—it's a cooking class, but for couples only. If you can't make it, I won't be able to check it out."

"You're checking out a cooking class for a bachelorette party?" he asked doubtfully.

"Yeah, it's a sexy class. Which is why I need a partner."

"Oh, well then…um, sure, I can come. What time?"

"Right now? As soon as you can get here?"

She closed her eyes, knowing she was asking a lot after turning down his invitation for the evening.

"Sounds fun. Where is it?"

She told him the address.

"I can be there in twenty minutes, so I'll see you soon."

They hung up and Della let go a sigh of relief. This was going to work, she just knew it.

Heading toward the kitchen, she waited for Gabe as long as possible until she was the last one outside in the hall. A guy in his twenties wearing a black suit gestured for her to enter, and she started to make an excuse, to wait for Gabe, just when he appeared at the end of the hall.

"Thank you for waiting a moment, there's my partner now," she said to the young man and smiling in Gabe's direction.

"Gabe, thank you so much for making it," she said with a quick hug and kiss, shuttling him in the door before they were both locked out.

The guy at the door introduced himself as Alex, and showed them to a tiny corner spot, where there was a table set with candles as well as a counter and cooking surface. Several bottles of wine and ingredients for mixed drinks lined a small bar behind the table. Five other couples had similar arrangements, three cooking/eating areas lined on either side of the room, with the cooking instruction table set at the front.

A widescreen TV by the cooking area would project the lesson, so that everyone could see and hear equally, with a red button that could be pressed for help or if they had questions.

"Wow, this is some setup," Gabe said under his breath.

"I wonder if they have a different setup for parties… it wouldn't be very festive to have everyone separate."

"You can ask later, I imagine. This is a great idea, though. What else did you consider?"

"I've been to every male strip club in Manhattan today, actually," she said, and grinned at the shock on his face. "It was educational, but I agree, I like this option better."

They both turned their attention to the front of the class, where two chefs—husband and wife, as they announced—introduced themselves and welcomed everyone to the class.

"The point of the evening is to have fun, to learn some of the seductive and aphrodisiac qualities of regular foods, and to make the time you spend in the kitchen with your partner a more intimate experience. Too often cooking becomes one person's *job* in a relationship, and that can lead to boring meals and the loss of a chance to connect with your significant other. But cooking, and food, are sensual experiences, and if you share the pleasures of the kitchen, you'll add a whole new layer of sensuality to your relationship, we promise," the female chef said, receiving an adoring look and a kiss on the cheek from her husband.

"There is one rule we like to add to our evening of

cooking—you must each share a secret with your partner while you are cooking, something you have never shared with them before."

Murmurs filled the room, and a few chuckles. Della wondered what secrets Gabe would share.

"And while touching and intimacy are encouraged, we keep it PG, please, and safe—we are using sharp knives and hot implements, so perhaps be discreet about which secrets you decide to share," the man said with a wink, and a shake of his spatula, making everyone laugh at the joke.

"The lesson starts with learning to move around each other in the kitchen space, and learning to share that space, which can be a dance of sorts. We're going to give you a list of tasks, which will show up on the screen above your counter. Get the job done, but find ways to touch, and to stand close to each other while you work, within reason, of course," the female chef instructed.

Then, the bustle of activity started, and she and Gabe were no exception, following the instructions on the screen while keeping an eye on the front of the room. Still, Della's focus was interrupted by how Gabe brushed by her, letting his arm graze her breast, or how he leaned in to kiss the back of her neck when he reached over her to get something from a cupboard.

For a second, her overachiever self, who took over when she was learning something, almost found that interruption annoying, but then she remembered why they were there. Two could play that game, she thought, as she watched him mixing the ingredients for dough that would become sweet rolls. He was confident in his movements, as if he was no stranger to the kitchen.

"This is fun," she said, sidling up next to him. Taking a moment from her own preparations, she stood behind him and pressed in, sliding her hands down his forearms until their hands met in the flour and moved over each other, kneading the soft dough together.

"Inhale the scents, notice the textures," the chef advised. "The aromas of the dough and the strawberries, whichever you are preparing, are both sensual and sweet, with known aphrodisiac qualities. Take time to experience every nuance."

As her hands moved with his, and her breasts pressed into his strong back, Della was noticing all the nuances she could handle, that was for sure. A few seconds later, she backed away, and washed her hands so that she could work on the strawberries. She noticed the ruddy color of arousal in Gabe's cheeks, though, and when he looked at her, it was reflected in his gaze.

"You keep that up, this dough isn't going to be the only thing rising," he said with a sideways grin, making her laugh out loud.

"I love it!" the female chef applauded in approval in their direction. "When you can laugh together, it's a beautiful thing."

Della nodded, returning her attention to the strawberries and following the directions for slicing them to perfection.

"Now follow the instructions for the glaze, and wrapping the fruit in the rolls with the honey glaze… and if you get a bit of honey on your partner, be sure to kiss it off," the female chef instructed with a mischievous tone.

As they assembled their sweet rolls, Gabe took some honey and rubbed it on her lip.

"Oh, sorry…let me get that for you," he said, and dipped in for a kiss, his tongue licking the sweet, sticky stuff from her lip.

It was all Della could do to keep her messy hands to herself, and not pull him closer for more.

When he pulled back, he smiled as he took in her expression, and she knew he could tell how much that kiss had affected her.

So turnabout was fair play, of course.

Taking an unsliced strawberry from her bowl, she didn't let her gaze leave his as she sank her teeth into it, licking the juice from her lips and then offering him the rest. As he bit into it, his mouth touching her fingertips, they both caught a breath.

"So what's your secret, Della?"

"Hmm?"

"We're supposed to share a secret. What's yours?"

Her mind scrambled. What secret could she share? Not that she had many of them.

"I… I've never had sex in a public place." She remembered the museum. "I mean, while the public was actually there."

That made his eyes glitter with particular interest.

"How about you? What's your secret?" she said as they finished their sweet rolls and moved on to the next course. For that, they simply had to create an herbed butter that they cooked over two steaks with salad. As instructed, she lifted the bouquet of herbs to her nose, inhaling the scent, though she didn't think she needed any help being turned on by Gabe.

Gabe didn't answer right away, but suddenly he turned serious as they cooked.

"I have only had one serious relationship in my whole life. I've only been in love once," he admitted.

Della's mouth went dry. She hadn't expected him to share something that important. She faced him, forgetting her food prep for the moment.

"What happened?"

By the look on his face, she knew it hadn't ended well.

"She died," he said, and put his knife down on the counter, shaking his head. "I'm sorry. It was all I could think of to share. That was a stupid thing to bring up here," he muttered, apologizing again as he took his apron off, leaving the cooking area.

Della followed him into the hall, abandoning the class. None of that mattered. Clearly Gabe had revealed something important, and she wanted to let him know it was okay. She also wanted to hear the rest of the story, if he would trust her enough to tell it.

8

GABE WAS LOSING IT—out in the quiet of the hall, he tried to think straight. Della had followed him, and now stood beside him, waiting quietly. She didn't push or prod, just waited.

"I'm sorry for ruining the fun," he said with a sigh. "I don't know why that came out just then, that way."

But he did know why.

It was because a part of him wanted her to know—that was the problem, what he had really wanted to say was that he'd only had one real relationship before now.

Before Della.

Thinking back to his feelings about Janet, as much as he'd thought he loved her, he couldn't remember ever being this crazy about someone, so much so that he was willing to chuck everything he believed in to be with her. Gabe had never completely lost objectivity until Della.

Worse, he was still tangled up in lies—big ones, and they were only getting bigger.

He'd lied, of course, to Bart, about being able to handle the situation with Della. He was lying to Della about an assortment of things—including that he had been following her that evening.

When she'd begged off of dinner with him, making vague excuses, he'd become suspicious. He'd planted a small tracking device in her bag and her coat when they were together last, so he could monitor her movements. He hadn't put surveillance in her home yet. He hadn't had the nerve.

Another problem.

After updating Bart on the fact that she'd been approached by her dance instructor, and that someone might have tried to assault her in her office, they both agreed that Gabe needed to stay as close as possible. That was the easy part. Getting too close was the danger, but Gabe had already crossed that line.

He'd watched her duck into several strip clubs, which didn't seem like her style, but how much did he really know about her? Maybe it was misdirection, or maybe it was a meet of some sort.

Then she was so open about it, that it was research for the bachelorette party, he'd been ashamed of his own suspicions. He thought he felt something more than sexual attraction for Della, but could he be suspicious of her yet lie to her at the same time when he thought he had serious feelings for her? Was that screwed up, or what?

Then his phone had rang, and it was Della. Asking him to meet her.

He had to make an excuse, stall, though he agreed—it wasn't like he could tell her he was right across the street.

Now, they stood quietly together in the hall, his

words hanging between them. She put a hand on his arm, a comforting, supportive gesture.

"It came up because you needed to say it, and I'm willing to listen, if you need to talk about it."

Another fork in the road.

Telling her about Janet meant something. It changed the game. And he had a job to do. Above all, was it fair to Della to drag her along, to make her feel like they had something real, when it was all smoke and mirrors?

"And if you don't, that's okay, too," she said simply, granting him the out.

Gabe fought the urge to come clean with her, to tell her everything and let the chips fall where they may.

As he started to speak, fate intervened as the door behind them opened and the female chef emerged, looking at them in concern.

"Oh, good, you're still here. We saw you leave, and I took the first chance I could to make sure you were okay. We thought someone might have gotten hurt," she said, her expression still worried.

"Oh, no, we're fine," Della reassured her. "We just needed a moment alone."

The chef's eyebrow raised curiously, the concern replaced with a spark of mischief.

"Oh, no," Della said, as Gabe watched her blush to the roots of her hair, which made him fight a smile. "We need to discuss something personal that came up."

The chef nodded. "I understand. Cooking together can spark all kinds of things, including the closeness necessary to share our innermost feelings. Though it's clear how you two feel about each other," she said with a wink. "If you want, I can help you catch up and enjoy the rest of the evening with us. I hope you will."

Gabe smiled, thankful for the rescue, and put his hand on Della's shoulder.

"We'd love to. Sorry for any disruption," he said.

"Wonderful!" she said, clearly pleased as she ushered them back to the cooking space, where she expertly chopped and chatted with them until they were caught up with the class.

"I like her. And her husband. I think this is definitely an option for the bachelorette party. Maybe I can ask them about doing some funny, sexy things, too."

"It's a great idea," Gabe agreed, leaning over to kiss her forehead as he put the salad on the table, and opened the bottle of wine recommended by the chefs.

As everyone sat down to eat their dinner, a crème brûlée cooked as they ate, adding to the delectable aromas filling the room.

"There really is something to cooking and the textures and aromas that can affect your mood and your mind-set," he said, somewhat surprised.

Della nodded, lifting a bite of her salad to his lips. One of the requirements of the class was also sharing your food, and feeding each other.

"I've read about it here and there, things like baking cookies or burning cinnamon candles when you want to sell your home, or to make people feel welcome," she said with a smile. "Our senses are so sharp, and yet we use them so carelessly most of the time."

"How so?"

"We don't pay attention, mostly, to everything around us. Sounds, scents, textures…how much gets lost in the rush of daily life?"

"That's true. But if we tried to take it all in, we'd never get anything done," he said with a grin.

Though he knew exactly how important it was to be a keen observer of his surroundings. In his world, what his senses told him could be the line between life and death.

Gabe cut a succulent bit of meat and, opting not to use the fork, offered it to her with his fingers, grazing her lips as she took the bite. Closing her eyes and inhaling as she chewed, he could only watch.

She was gorgeous.

"Oh, that's amazing," she said on a half sigh, and he knew she didn't mean only the steak as her eyes opened and met his.

The touch of her mouth to his fingertips as he offered her a second bite sent sparks of arousal skittering over his skin. He pulled back, disconcerted. He wanted her, but it was almost overwhelming. Gabe wasn't accustomed to being overwhelmed. By anything. Anyone.

She sent him reeling out of control over and over again, and he didn't like *that*. Didn't like saying things he didn't mean to say, or dealing with emotions that he didn't want to feel.

"Gabe?" she asked, half-cautious, half-worried.

He focused, shoved his feelings down. Smiled.

"Sorry, you sent my mind elsewhere… For instance, wondering what we could do in this small, *public* space," he said, inching his chair closer to hers.

Leaning in, he put his mouth close to her ear. "What could I get away with in this room full of people, Della? What could I do to you with all of them just yards away?"

He felt her shiver as his hand found her knee, slid up under the edge of her skirt.

She looked over her shoulder, past him, toward the room where everyone was sitting, the chefs making the rounds to spend a little time with each couple. They were several tables away, and the cooking counter offered some privacy, if not much.

Gabe slid his hand higher, as his other lifted his wine to take a drink before sharing the taste with Della via a kiss.

"Do you want me to stop?" he asked, resting his hand between her thighs, enjoying the heat he discovered there. She wore tights, but that was hardly a barrier.

She swallowed hard, closing her eyes as he rubbed, and shook her head.

Gabe's heart sped as he found an intimate spot that made her bite her lip in response.

"Shhh…no one can know. And the chefs will be here in just a few minutes," he said, turning so he could palm her breast with his other hand, thumbing the hard point with just enough pressure to make her shudder.

"You need to come, Della… I want you to come," he whispered, increasing the pressure of his touch in both spots until her head dropped against his shoulder, her entire frame tightening and then releasing as she did just as he asked her.

The pulse in her neck raced, her cheeks flushed, eyes hazy as he removed his hand, smoothed her skirt.

Anyone looking at her would know what just happened.

Maybe anyone looking at him would know the same, that for the moment, he had retained control. Had managed to play the game and not lose his way.

Until she took a drink of her wine, catching her

breath and calming down, before she turned the tables, her hand sliding into *his* lap.

The chefs laughed, their voices closer now, only one table away. Gabe was already hard from making her come, and it took every ounce of that self-control he valued so much to lift her hand away as their teachers approached their table.

As they visited and shared their compliments about the class, Gabe was impressed with how Della rallied, not appearing flustered at all. For all anyone knew, the flush in her cheeks was from the wine. She discussed the bachelorette party, and had locked down the date before the couple moved on.

"When you decide to do something, you don't waste any time, do you?"

"Not when I know it's the right decision."

Gabe nodded. How often had he been that certain of anything? Not often…at least, not recently.

"I feel pretty sure about something else, too," she said mischievously.

"What's that?"

"While what you just did was sort of like having sex in public, it wasn't *really* having sex. It was one-sided, and just a warm-up. An…appetizer," she said flirtatiously.

What was she getting at?

Taking his hand, her eyes sparkled as she led him to the back, where everyone had left their coats, bags and briefcases.

The coat closet?

"Della, I really don't think we should—"

As she pulled him inside and closed the door, she

put her back against the door as she beckoned him to join her.

"You're experienced enough at covert operations to carry this off, don't you think?" she teased, peeling off her tights and shoving them in her bag.

Gabe didn't want to resist, though he knew he should. She had a way of turning things around, making him throw caution to the wind.

As he leaned into her, his hands planted on the door on either side of her head, she unzipped his pants, her nimble fingers closing around him and stealing his words before he could object again. Five minutes later, deep inside of her, Gabe forgot whatever objections he had.

DELLA MISSED GABE.

She knew that she shouldn't, but the past week had been so marvelous, it was hard not to feel his absence. But she was an independent, modern woman, determined not to pine over the absence of a lover.

Today, she'd focused on her work, meeting with new grad students coming into the program in the fall and then with Chloe to help with final wedding arrangements and a light dinner.

Having gone through her life pretty much alone as a young person, Della knew the value of her friends, and she wasn't going to ignore them just because she was with a guy. That was rule number one.

No matter how great that guy was.

Still, Gabe had been on her mind almost constantly in spite of her best intentions, and every time she checked her phone and found no message from him, her heart sank a bit.

Grow up, Della. He also had responsibilities and maybe he had decided to focus on his work today, too. He'd said she was a distraction, after all, she thought with a smile.

She'd never been told that before.

"How is it going with lover boy?" Chloe asked as they strode up the steps to Della's apartment. "You haven't mentioned him all afternoon, but you've checked your phone a million times. Trouble in paradise?"

Della stalled, unsure how to respond as she grabbed her mail and picked through it, separating the junk from the things she wanted.

"Della?"

"Sorry. No, there's no trouble. I don't think so, anyway. We've had the best week, actually. Yet I can't help but feel the hovering of that other shoe about to drop—this wasn't supposed to be a long-term relationship, and that hasn't changed. Not that I know of."

"He hasn't suggested otherwise?"

Della frowned and leaned back against the wrought-iron rail on her stoop. "That's where it feels muddy. I know he can't share a lot about his job, but I can't help feeling that it's more than that."

"Like what?"

Della sat on the cast-iron bench that she'd put on her stoop, and Chloe joined her.

"I don't know. Like he wants to maintain a certain distance, especially if he feels like we're getting too close? He'll let his guard down for a second, but then if I ask anything too personal, he clams up. He almost shared with me about a relationship he had before, a serious one—the woman died."

"Oh, how awful!"

Della nodded, looking down at her hands. "It is. But then he clammed up and never mentioned it again, and I don't feel right asking, though I'm curious, of course. And since that moment, while he's sweet and attentive about sex, that's pretty much all it seems we have."

"Hmm. Except on your side, I take it? You have more feelings for him?"

"I could, if I let myself. I wonder, if he lost someone he really loved, if he's ever going to want to be with anyone else. Maybe that's why he keeps things temporary and light. And I know I should, too, but it's difficult."

"Or, maybe you should tell him how you feel…who knows? Maybe he needs to hear that. If he is gun-shy, maybe he needs a push?"

"I don't know that I'd like his response."

"That is always the risk," Chloe agreed with a sigh, as Della slid the key in the lock of her door, but the door pushed open on its own.

"What the heck?" she whispered to herself. She was positive she had locked her door, and double-checked it. She always did.

"Della, stop," Chloe said sharply and put a stern hand on her shoulder.

Della was startled, and then realized her friend's wisdom; she had to be cautious about stepping inside her home if the door was open. Someone could still be there.

Sudden fear chilled her to the bone, especially since she had been ignoring her feelings of being followed, believing that she was being paranoid. Maybe not.

"I'm calling the police before we set foot in there," Chloe said.

Della, as much as she wanted to go inside her home, agreed.

Minutes later, a squad car arrived, and Della stood outside with Chloe, anxious as the officers disappeared inside her home, guns drawn.

After a few minutes, they reappeared, their weapons holstered, although they looked grim.

"You're the owner of the home?" they asked Della.

She nodded, her heart in her throat.

"Well, no one is in there, it's safe to enter, but I hate to tell you that the place is trashed. You should brace yourself for that before you go inside. Also, be careful where you step, and don't touch anything."

"Trashed?" Della said incredulously. "You mean someone wrecked my things?"

"That's putting it mildly."

Chloe's hand landed on her shoulder in support, and Della needed it. Her knees were so shaky she wasn't sure she could take a step.

Still, her legs carried her back up the steps and to the door, where she went inside, needing to see how bad it was. Standing in her entryway, she let out a small cry.

It was very bad.

"Who would do this?" Chloe whispered from behind her, sounding equally shocked.

"Have you had any trouble lately? An ex-boyfriend or someone you might have had an altercation with?" the older officer asked.

Della shook her head, and then stopped. "I was at my office one night and I thought someone followed me, but that ended up being nothing."

Or so she thought.

"Anything else?"

Della fought tears, taking in the slashed leather furniture, the toppled tables and emptied drawers. Antiques were broken, frames were taken from the walls, where some holes had been punched into the plaster. That was going to be expensive to fix, she thought vaguely. Did insurance cover damage from break-ins? One of her stained-glass lamp shades was shattered, and there was so much more she could barely take it all in. It was a feast of destruction.

"Della? The officer asked if anything else has happened recently?" Chloe said gently.

She quaked from head to toe, and nodded. "Nothing specific, but the past few days, I kept feeling like someone was watching me, but I thought I was being overly anxious after what happened at my office."

"Okay, that's not much to go on. This could have been random. We'll have a car come by here regularly over the next couple of days and evenings. You should change the locks right away, and luckily the windows are in one piece. You may want to stay with a friend or at a hotel for a few days, and be sure to report anything unusual."

"I'll change the locks today, but I'm staying here," she said more to herself than the policeman. "This is my home."

The officer nodded before rejoining his partner.

Chloe was concerned, too. "Della, you should stay with us. Justin won't mind, I promise. You don't know if this person will come back—this isn't your ordinary break-in. It's so...violent," she said, looking around again, as horrified as Della was, too.

She stumbled into the midst of the mess, still in shock. But as she went through her home, she started to see a sort of shape to the madness.

"It's as if they were searching for something," she said to Chloe. "See how things are opened up…emptied out? They didn't just slash the furniture, they pulled out the stuffing. Why? The holes in the walls are at intervals."

Chloe shook her head. "What could they have been looking for? That doesn't make any sense. Maybe they thought you hid money or valuables in those places?"

Della frowned and headed upstairs to find that space less disrupted, though it was clear someone had still rifled through her drawers and closets—perhaps they ran out of time? But why would anyone search and destroy her home?

"Della, please. Come stay with us until this is cleaned up, at least. Justin and I will come over tomorrow and help you start putting it all back together. He can probably repair the holes in the wall—he's good at that kind of thing. It's the least we can do for all the help you've been with the wedding."

Della put a hand to her forehead. "Oh, the wedding! There are still so many last-minute things I need to check."

Chloe put both hands on Della's shoulders and turned her toward her, making eye contact. "Forget that, it's not important. Everything is more or less set to go, and it will be fine. I'll wrap up any loose ends. But I insist you stay with us until your apartment is back to rights."

Della nodded. "Maybe that would be best. Listen, you go ahead, and I can pack some things and come over later. Right now, I'd like to call Gabe and have him come check this out before we touch anything, and I need to get a locksmith here, too."

"I'm not leaving you alone here."

"I'll be fine, Chloe, seriously. I'll call when I'm on my way."

Obviously not happy about the plan, but knowing she wasn't going to change Della's mind, Chloe nodded. "Okay, well, I'm at least going to wait until we know Gabe is on his way over."

Della hugged her overprotective friend and took out her phone, relieved that Gabe answered immediately and told her he'd be there right away.

True to his word, just moments after Chloe left, Gabe appeared on her porch, knocking and taking her immediately in his arms when she greeted him.

Yes. This was what she needed, she thought, as his warmth infused her. Her mind calmed and she stepped back so that he could see the extent of the damage.

"It's pretty hard to believe, isn't it? Who would want to do this to me? The police thought maybe an angry student, or a stalker, but... I just find that so hard to believe."

"It's pretty thorough, I'll say that."

Gabe's expression turned to stone as he looked around, his thoughts inscrutable if not for a flash of anger that darkened his eyes from hazel to a deep brown.

Della rubbed her arms as she stood at his side.

"But they said it could also be random."

Gabe stepped into the main room...passing by the sofa where they had made love for the first time. He walked upstairs for a few minutes, and then came back down.

"No, I don't think so."

"How can you tell?"

"They didn't take any of the art or the valuables, your TV, computer…in fact, many of your electronics are untouched. It was meant to look violent, angry, or like garden-variety vandalism, but it's not. Too much of the same thing, in each room…they went after the furniture, things that would break and make a mess. The upstairs was rifled a bit, but most of the destruction is down here, like it's staged to shock you when you open the door. It was meant to be upsetting."

Della huffed out a breath. "Well, it is certainly that. I thought it looked like…they were trying to find something?"

"Do you have any idea what? Do you keep valuables hidden here?"

"No, not really. Nothing that would call for this, unless they had the wrong house. Maybe that's why they stopped by the time they got upstairs, they might have realized that whatever they wanted wasn't here?"

Gabe shook his head. "I doubt it—it's meant to scare you. But why would someone go to these lengths to do that?"

Della thought about her pursuer at the school.

"Like at my office. Nothing happened, but it just freaked me out. I've felt like I've been being followed for days, but I assumed I was imagining things. It's been making me a little crazy, though."

A flicker of something odd moved over his features, but only for a second.

"Fairly typical stalker behavior, actually. Any conflicts at work, with a student, a co-worker? An ex?"

"I had one student who was disappointed I couldn't work with him on his thesis, and he was unhappy, but not *this* unhappy—and why would he wait two months to react?"

"Valid point, but give me his name and I'll check up on him, just in case. This is the kind of passive-aggressive thing someone might do when they don't have the courage to confront you themselves, though it can escalate."

"Escalate?" she asked nervously.

"Let's take care of one thing at a time. Did you touch anything, or the police?"

"No."

"Okay, good. I'll get someone in here to dust for prints and see if that tells us anything for starters. I can call someone in tonight."

"Oh, the police said they don't usually do that unless there was a death, or a physical attack."

Gabe caught her eye. "I'm not the police."

"Of course, yes. Thank you." She crossed the room to hug him, and took comfort in his strength.

There was a knock at the door, and Della jumped. Her nerves really were on edge. Looking out the window, she saw the locksmith's van.

"Great, they're here to change the locks." She left Gabe to make his calls as she met the locksmiths and let them get to work, before rejoining Gabe.

"You can't stay here tonight. Especially, not if I have a team come in. It might be smart to stay elsewhere, anyway, to get a room a few miles away, for a while, maybe a week or so, to be on the safe side."

"Chloe and Justin said I could stay with them, but honestly, I hate to intrude, and I like my time alone. But I don't want them to have hurt feelings, so I agreed."

He frowned. "It's too easy, if there is someone after

you, to know who your friends are, and that you would go stay with them."

Della's eyes widened. She'd never thought of that.

"Right. I can't risk bringing any danger to their door. That makes it an easy decision. I will definitely book a room."

"You could stay with me."

She peered up at him a bit apprehensively. "Thank you, that means a lot, but I'd rather be closer to my apartment, since I need to put things back to rights and you're way downtown. But…will you stay tonight? I mean, at the hotel? With me?"

He hesitated for a second, which made her almost regret asking.

"Of course. I can do that, and I'll tell my team to check in. Hopefully we'll know something by morning."

She wondered why he hadn't said yes right away, but was too exhausted to give it much thought. "They shouldn't be long with the lock. I'll go make some calls and pack a case."

Della turned to go upstairs, and Gabe caught her hand, pulled her back in for a moment, his mouth by her ear.

"It will be okay, Della. I won't let anyone hurt you. No matter what this is about."

She lifted her face to his, offering a kiss, which he took, then she went to pack. He'd had that strange expression again, she thought, as she grabbed her clothes. Protective, but also…secretive. Like he was holding something back.

Della shook the thought away. Gabe didn't deserve her suspicions. Fear was making her suspicious of everything, and everyone. He'd come to help right away, even though he had his own very important work to do.

She dropped an email to Chloe about her changed plans, and then took her case back downstairs to meet Gabe and wait for the locksmith to finish up so she could leave.

"I'll stay at the hotel for a few days, but I'm coming back to fix up my place as soon as you're done," she said to Gabe, feeling more solid as she took one of her new keys and gave it to him to let his team inside. "This is my home, and I'm not being run out of it."

"I wouldn't expect anything else, Della, and if there's anything else I can do to help, just say so," he told her as he put his arm around her shoulders and pulled her closer.

For now, it was everything Della could ask.

9

"THE MISSION'S OVER, GABE. It's done."

Gabe leaned back in his office chair in shock. After he'd left Della at the hotel the night before, sleeping soundly, he'd gone back to her place, and then to his office that morning, to find a message from Bart with orders to stop the interviews and pull the surveillance on Petroski.

The lab had given up all of the files and data on the formula to DHS, and it was being transferred to another secure location. Even the scientists he was supposed to interview had gone.

"What do you mean, it's done?"

Bart's tone was not apologetic.

"Orders came down from over both our heads, Gabe. With no solid leads and an increasing threat of another attempt by Derian to get the formula, we couldn't risk him succeeding. I got orders to shut the project down and get the formula and the staff off-site to a secure location. Petroski was fired. If Derian is out there, he's been cut off."

Gabe's head reeled with the news.

"So what now?"

"Well, your investigation into the leak is done, but the mission is far from over."

"How so?"

"What happened at Dr. Clark's? Any leads?"

"No, nothing useful."

"What's your take on it?"

"The job was professional, though it was meant to look otherwise. But they left no prints, nada. Someone made sure it was staged, clean. They knew what they were doing. But what I can't figure out is why. It's like it was meant to scare her."

"A message, perhaps? Could be Derian is panicked, and letting his people know he's not backing down?"

"Perhaps, but I don't think she's knowingly involved. She was genuinely surprised, afraid. If she's in this, she's being used in some way."

It had cut deep to have to look Della in the eye and pretend like he knew nothing when she admitted she felt as if she had been followed. It had been difficult to let her think someone was after her, especially when he was the one doing the following. But he couldn't tell her the truth. Increasingly, he wanted to, though. He'd come close, that night at her apartment.

"That brings us to the change in your mission. We still want Derian. If you think Dr. Clark is the best lead we have on him, then stick with her. See if she draws him out."

Gabe stiffened at the suggestion. "Wait…you want to use Della, Dr. Clark, as bait? She's a civilian, Bart—"

"We've used civilians before."

"With their knowledge and consent. Della has given neither. I should read her in."

"Absolutely not. If you're wrong, she'll tip off Derian. If you're right, she could blow the whole thing. You stick with her and see if he shows. Or any of his men. He might not do his own dirty work, I imagine."

"At this point, we don't even know for sure that he's there, and with the formula out of play, maybe he's gone."

"No, he wouldn't leave without scorching the earth behind him. If it's not her, maybe it's someone close to her, someone she knows. This is the angle now. We want Derian, that's the mission."

Gabe closed his eyes. "If we get him, we can find out who he was working for."

"Bingo. And if the good doctor can help us with that, then consider her in protective custody. Yours."

There was a pause, and Gabe said, "And if it turns out she's not involved? What if he's not the one after her?"

"No harm, no foul. You pack up, come back, get your next assignment."

"How long?"

"If Derian is going to make a move, he's going to make it sooner than later. I'll give it until the end of the week. If he doesn't make a move by then, then you're back here, new assignment."

Bart hung up and Gabe was left staring at the phone. He badly wanted to hit something, anger and frustration a knot in his gut.

He'd been lying to Della all of this time, and now he had to knowingly put her in the path of danger? Use her again? Without her knowledge?

At least he could keep her safe—and he would. But only for this week? What about after that? His stomach went sour at the thought, but Bart was right. He'd done it before, but this was Della. This was different.

And yet, he really had no choice. Derian was a dangerous criminal, and if he was anywhere near Della, or behind what had been happening to her, Gabe was going to make sure he was between the terrorist and her. He couldn't be there to protect Janet, but he'd be damned if he would walk away from Della before he knew—completely—that she was safe.

He left the office, thinking about how to approach Della now that his job was, in fact, her. He'd promised Della he wouldn't let anyone hurt her, and it was a promise he intended to keep. He could continue to follow her, when she thought he was working, but that left a bad taste in his mouth, knowing how vulnerable she felt.

She'd mentioned a morning meeting at the university—that even though it wasn't the school term, professors still had administration. She'd promised not to leave the campus until he returned.

Looking out the eighth-story window at the sun blazing down on the pavement, he watched people trudging along through the intense heat. They'd predicted over-the-top temperatures for the entire weekend.

With that thought, an idea formed.

He could keep a close eye on Della while potentially taking her out of the line of danger for a few days if they went out of town. Both of them could use a break.

Or, another way to look at it was that if someone *was* keeping tabs on her, other than him, then that person would be a lot easier to spot outside of the city.

Gabe's mind was made up. He did some internet

searches, made a few phone calls and set out to meet Della at the university.

Anticipation lightened his step, even though he was still technically on the job. He couldn't let his guard down—Derian could appear at anytime—but he couldn't help but look forward to more time with Della.

He grabbed a cab, not wanting to wait for a train, and new energy filled him as he walked across the quad toward Della's building. But as he crossed the large quad, he saw her in conversation with a tall man, longish hair, muscular build. The guy was standing far too close, in Gabe's estimation. Della stepped back slightly, but the man drew closer.

All of his senses went on alert, and Gabe's walk changed to a jog as he approached them.

"Della," he said loudly, making both she and the man talking to her turn.

"Gabe, hi," she said, her expression clearly relieved when she saw him.

Which meant whoever this guy was, he wasn't welcome company.

"Gabe, this is Steven. I mentioned him to you—he's one of the teachers in my dance class," she said, her tone overly polite, strained.

Steven didn't look happy and faced Gabe with a pointed glare.

"We were talking," he said rudely, turning away from Gabe.

"I think that Della is done talking to *you*," Gabe said smoothly, looking in her direction for confirmation. Steven didn't bear any resemblance to Derian, but Gabe wasn't taking any chances—the guy could be one of his associates, keeping an eye on Della.

"Listen, buddy—"

Gabe closed in. "I'm not your buddy, and you were just leaving. You will leave the lady alone, period."

Steven blustered, focusing on Della.

"Does he speak for you now?"

Della crossed her arms in front of her, but looked quite piqued.

"No, but he's right. I don't have anything else to say. I'm not interested in dating you, and I meant that. I'm sorry."

"Apparently you're just a tease," Steven sneered, backing up and giving Gabe a dirty, but wary, glance as he stormed off.

Della leaned back against the door, and only then did Gabe notice how pale and tired she looked. She'd had a hell of a couple of days, and suddenly he doubted his idea to take off for the weekend. Maybe she had things to do or wouldn't appreciate his making plans for them.

"I guess that's the end of my dance lessons, which is fine with me, but still. What is going on in my life? People break into my apartment, and then Steven was waiting outside my office when I came out. He was just…lurking, and scared the life out of me. I thought he might be whoever chased me before."

"Do you think that's possible?"

She shrugged. "I don't know what to think, but he sure wasn't as charming as he always was in class. What a creep. I didn't call him back, so he decided to find me at work, he said. I walked him all the way down here hoping he would leave, but he just kept pushing, wanting to know why I didn't come to class today, and when I would go out with him," she said, shaking her head. "He said I was avoiding him. I was so glad to see you coming toward us I can't even tell you how much. I was about to call campus security again."

"I'm glad I showed up at the right time. Are you sure you're okay?"

She nodded. "Just tired. And annoyed. I didn't sleep so well last night, thinking about the break-in, and that I might have a stalker. Maybe I'm being overly harsh about Steven because of that, but he really freaked me out."

"You're a nice person, Della, but you never need to be nice to a guy who can't take no for an answer the first time."

She smiled weakly at him. "Thank you. I know. Anyway…it's good to see you."

"You, too. I have the results from your apartment. Unfortunately, no prints or any leads. It may well have been random vandalism."

"That's so disconcerting."

"I know, but I promise I'll keep looking into it."

"Thank you," she said, squinting up at the sky. "It's *so* hot. I knew they predicted a heat wave this weekend, but this is even more intense than I expected."

"Yeah, about that," he said, feeling even less certain than he had earlier. "I was thinking…do you want to get out of town for the weekend? I rented a car and I thought maybe we could head upstate, into the mountains, where it will be cooler."

"What about your work?"

"The investigation is winding down. I can take a few days off."

"Oh." She broke eye contact, staring down at the

sidewalk before shifting her gaze back to him. "Does that mean you're leaving?"

He knew what she meant, though her tone was neutral, pleasant. That this was the end of their affair. That the weekend away was a goodbye of sorts.

In a way, he wished it was—that would be more honest.

Gabe stepped in, put his hands on her shoulders, looking her square in the eye. "I'm not going anywhere until I know you're safe. Promise. This weekend is just…a lark. I could use a break, too."

She smiled up at him. "Getting out of the city does sound lovely, but the break-in, and the mess… I should start cleaning it all up, and the wedding prep. It's next Friday, you know. The bachelorette party is set, and they have planned the rehearsal dinner themselves, but I feel like I should be here in case Chloe needs me."

"She'd understand. It's only a few days. Tell her you need to get away, but if she needs you, she can call or email."

Gabe let the front of his body brush hers, watched her cheeks flush from more than the heat of the day.

"Three days alone, in the mountains, in a cabin. By a very cool, pretty lake. What do you say?"

Della groaned, but the sparkle returned to her eyes and she nodded. "That sounds amazing. And I already have my bag packed at the room. When did you want to go?"

"I have to pick up the car, then my bag, and we're out of here. Let's go by your place first? It's only a four-hour drive upstate."

Her smile widened, and she planted a hand on his chest, biting her lip in an enticing way.

"We'll be all alone in a cabin by a lake, huh? What will there be to do for three days?"

Gabe grinned back, leaning in closer to steal a kiss. "Oh, I'm sure we'll think of something."

DELLA WORKED OUT three times a week, or she tried to, anyway, but none of that had prepared her for hiking up the steep path they had chosen for their daily outing. No one would have guessed that the softly curved Adirondack Mountains would provide such a challenge. It hadn't looked this steep from the bottom, but the copse of thick trees hid the real challenge.

Of course, it could be that while she'd slept like the dead the night before, lulled by the cool mountain air, cricket songs and amazing sex, her physical activities and stress lately had taken a toll.

That's my excuse, and I'm sticking to it, she thought, smirking as she took in Gabe's strong stride as he ambled along a few feet ahead of her. He wasn't even breaking a sweat, though she imagined how hot he would look all sweaty, and felt a ripple of desire thrum through her.

It only got stronger, the more time they spent together. Maybe that meant this weekend was a mistake, but for now, she didn't care.

Admiring the wide expanse of his back, and how it narrowed down to his lean hips and very cute backside, she couldn't complain about the view as she pushed herself along. Then he stopped, pointing to a large, flat boulder shaded from the sun, looking out over the forest below.

"I could use a break. Looks like a good spot for lunch?" he asked.

"You won't get an argument from me." Della tried not to huff and puff her answer. Sitting down for a while sounded like heaven.

They walked together to the spot, and Gabe swung off the backpack he'd volunteered to carry for them both like it weighed nothing at all. Handing her the blanket they'd brought from the cabin, she shook it out and made a place for them to sit.

Gabe stood at the edge of the boulder and looked out over the wilderness, quiet for a moment as Della dove into the pack, retrieving the lunch they had had packed for them at one of the cafés in the local town. When he didn't sit, she looked up.

"You okay?"

He turned, moving over to join her.

"I'm great, sorry. Just was lost in thought. I forgot how much I love being out in the middle of nowhere like this. It's like leaving the world behind."

"I know. I don't get out of the city much, except to go to different cities, for work. A few times, I went with a group of friends to upstate farms in the fall for apples or pumpkins, and things like that, but not often. When you're in the city, it can seem like you have everything you need, it's all right there, except for this. Fresh air, open space…it's wonderful. Thank you for arranging it," she said, looking up into his face.

His features were so relaxed. Happy, which made him even handsomer. And sexier. As a little ripple of heat moved through her, she sighed. She couldn't seem to get enough of him.

"You're welcome. This food looks great, I'm starving. Let's eat," he said voraciously.

"They really did give us a lot." She noted the wide

array of sandwiches, cheese, chips, fruit and drinks. "I think the café lady who was flirting with you packed a little extra."

"Good thing," he said, digging into one of the sandwiches while Della ate some cheese and an apple.

"Do you do this often, hike out in the mountains?"

"I used to. We grew up in Denver, and the Rockies were our playground. My brother and I spent most of our time climbing or hiking from the time we were kids. My parents met on an expedition team climbing Kilimanjaro, so they raised us in the same tradition. In fact, they're spending this summer in the Andes. It sounds pretty amazing, from their emails."

"Wow, I'm impressed. That explains why this is literally like a walk in the park for you while I'm barely keeping up."

"City girl," he teased, his eyes crinkling at the corners as he smiled at her. "You're doing fine. I guess I missed it more than I thought. The air, the exercise. Work takes over. Maybe too much."

She nodded in agreement, her appetite spiking as she reached for more goodies.

"My parents are more urban types," she said in kind. "They travel widely, always did. Very focused on culture and history. They took me along when they could, but a lot of my time when I was young was focused on school."

"No siblings, I take it?"

"Just me. Are you close with your brother?"

Gabe's expression turned strained. "We always have been, but not as much lately. My fault entirely. We haven't seen each other for almost two years now, though we stay in touch on email, the occasional phone call. Still, he and his wife had a second baby last January, and I've only seen pictures."

Della reached over, put her hand on his arm. "You sound like you miss them. Don't DHS agents get holidays off?"

"Sure, but I didn't take the time. Not for the past two holidays, anyway. There were…other things going on. I wasn't in the right head space to be around family."

She sensed the mood had changed, and Gabe stopped eating, staring back out over the tree line.

"Was that because the woman you were telling me about, the one you were involved with, died?"

Della held her breath, hoping she wasn't stepping over a line and possibly ruining their weekend, but she couldn't help it. The question had been at the back of her thoughts since he'd brought it up before. Clearly it was an event that had moved him deeply.

Several moments passed, and Gabe didn't take his eyes off the view as he spoke. "About two years ago, yes. I guess I'd lost track of that, too, which is what I intended. I just didn't pay attention to anything else."

Della was quiet, hoping that would invite him to say more. She also didn't want to push. Whatever he shared with her, it had to be his decision.

"Her name was Janet, and we were partners since I started at the DHS. She had slightly more seniority. *That* she never let me forget," he said with a rueful grin. "But I had a lot more experience."

"How long were you together?"

"Three years. We only became lovers six months before she was killed. I suppose that wasn't very long, but…it really pulled the rug out from under me. Maybe because we had history, or because I wasn't there for her when she needed me. I couldn't get my head around it for a long time, that she was gone. Even though she wasn't the first person I knew who had been lost in the line of duty, it was…harder."

"She was special to you, so obviously it would be different. What happened? What do you mean that you weren't there for her?"

He leaned back on his elbow, looking at her now, blowing out a breath before he spoke again. His fingers absently played with a small stone he picked up.

"We'd been following a money-laundering operation for a while, investigating bogus business fronts that were moving cash to terrorist cells in the US and other allied countries. We were gathering enough evidence to send in multi-agency strike teams, trying to follow the path to the source as far as we could. The goal was to get as many of the major players as possible. The people operating the businesses were small fish—we wanted the guys running the show."

Della nodded.

"It was mostly background work, surveillance and research. Then my department sent me to Africa to help with a problem with an operation there, and there was no reason to think Janet couldn't handle things here on her own. But then something broke, and they had a small window to get in and grab a major player who had suddenly shown up on the radar in D.C. She went in with the strike team, but things went bad. She was shot, fatally. And that was that. I didn't even know she was gone until I was on my way home. I almost missed the funeral," he said, his voice low, soft. Laced with regret.

It was easy to see it was still painful for him.

"No one told you? They didn't wait?"

"Protocol. DHS couldn't risk compromising the work I was doing in Africa, and her family had no idea about me, so they had scheduled the funeral quickly. Also, I found out shortly afterward there was a mole. Someone had told the terrorists that the strike team was coming—it was the only way they could have been taken out so easily. They even thought it might be me at first. It was a huge mess."

Della was shocked beyond words that one of Gabe's own people was responsible for what had happened.

"That's unbelievable."

"I couldn't believe it, either, at first. When I returned, and she was gone... I don't know. It was like I turned my back for a minute and the world changed. I didn't react well—especially when they took me off the case altogether."

"Oh, Gabe, I'm so sorry. What a terrible thing to go through."

"I found out about the mole—a buddy told me, off the record—and I started investigating, off-book, which was why they benched me in the first place, turns out. Bart figured he might as well put me in there undercover, since I was going to do it anyway, once I knew. I had to. I owed that much to her. But it was perfect, since everyone thought I'd been put on leave, their guard was down."

She held her breath at the predatory look in his eye, the razor-sharp intent. Della had no doubt he'd accomplished his task.

"You found him?"

He nodded, but seemed calm, more serene than she would expect.

"I did. Not a he, though. One of Janet's team, someone she trusted and confided in. That's how they knew what she was up to. She's serving a life sentence now. I wanted to do worse, but unfortunately, she didn't give me an excuse. Government employees aren't paid a lot, so she was padding her retirement fund by leaking information to the enemies. On several operations, it turned out."

The words were delivered coolly, matter-of-factly, and made her shiver even on the warm summer day.

"I'm glad that you found her."

Della also understood, now, why he only wanted casual associations, like the one they had. The fact that his lover hadn't been able to trust her best friend, and that had led to her death—how could Gabe ever trust anyone, living in a world like he did? Where you couldn't even trust the people who were supposed to have your back?

If Della thought she had problems connecting with others, in forming relationships, she could only imagine how difficult it would be for him. Casual was the only way to function in that case. Easy come, easy go, because you never knew what was going to happen next.

Though, the way her heart hurt for him just then, she had to admit that their relationship was becoming less and less casual, at least for her. Still, that was her problem. He had never promised anything more.

"Thank you for confiding in me," she said, moving closer to him, her palm cupping his cheek as she leaned in for a soft kiss. Though his pain was in the past—or was it?—she was moved by the urge to comfort, and to connect. To take off the chill that had come over them. To let him know that for this moment, anyway, he wasn't alone. That until he left, she wasn't going anywhere.

The kiss lingered, and he moved some of their food out of the way so that he could pull her closer, investigating the depths of her mouth more deeply, making her heart hammer in her chest. Della's fingers slipped up underneath the edge of his T-shirt, moving across the taut skin of his waist, and she felt his arm around her tighten.

His lips slid to her ear and he mumbled, "Keep that up, and we're going to have to add a second public place to your resume," as he nipped the lobe and made her catch her breath.

She pulled back slightly to check behind them.

"I don't see anyone around." Her eyes met his with mischievous challenge and he smiled, pulling her in for another kiss.

"Temptress," he accused softly, his hand moving to her breast. The thin material of the tank top she wore was almost no barrier at all to the heat of his hand and the teasing of his fingers.

Two could play that game, she thought, her fingers finding him, hard and ready, and sliding into his shorts to close around him. He groaned, encouraging her with a slight movement of his hips.

"I love how you make me feel," she said against his mouth as his hands dipped lower, too, making her shudder against him.

"Tell me."

Sensations were stealing her breath as she searched for the right words. "Wild…like I really am sexy, and daring."

"You are all of those things, Della, and more," he whispered, pausing to look at her intently.

"Not before...not with anyone else," she admitted as his touch made her close her eyes and fight the urge to cry out, just in case anyone was close by.

"I can't say I'm not happy about that," he said, his tone rough, his breath short as she pushed him to the edge, too. "But you shouldn't doubt yourself. You... move me, too. Deeply."

She thrilled to those words, and they made her bolder. Reaching for the zipper of his shorts, Della decided she had other plans for Gabe. She wanted to wipe out any bad memory as well as any clear thought he had in his head, and it excited her to realize she was capable of doing exactly that.

But as she kissed him once and started to move down his body, his hand squeezed her shoulder, making her still.

Then she heard it, not too close, but audible, the laughter and voices of others. They weren't alone.

"We should probably pack up and head on," he said.

Della's frustration was obvious, but he sat up, pulled her up with him, tipping her face up to his.

"Suddenly the summit is a lot less interesting now. Want to head back to our cabin? Maybe go for a swim in the lake?"

That conjured all kinds of wonderful images and possibilities in Della's mind, and she couldn't agree fast enough. And as they fixed their clothes and collected the remainder of their lunch, the voices came closer, a tour group of young scouts appearing on the path above them, and Della had to let go of a sigh of relief.

"Good decision to stop," she told Gabe with a rueful grin. "We would have spent the rest of the day in jail for public indecency."

He chuckled as they headed in the opposite direction of the group, back down the path. Della felt reenergized and moved a lot faster now, keeping pace with Gabe, because she couldn't wait to get him alone for a bit of private indecency, she thought to herself with a grin.

Her time with him might be limited, and was likely drawing to a close, but she pushed that thought to the back of her mind, intent on enjoying every second they had left. Hopefully, leaving both of them with some good memories. After Gabe was gone, she had a feeling she would need those as much as he would.

10

GABE DOVE FROM the dock, cutting through the clear water of the mountain lake, loving the way the cold shocked his senses. Breaking the surface, he looked up at Della, who still stood on the dock that ran out in front of their cabin, dipping a toe in doubtfully.

"It's not that cold once you're in, I promise," he said with as much sincerity as he could muster.

It was actually pretty darned cold, but in a good way. The sweat and heat from the hike and the sun seemed to simply evaporate from his body. Though the heat he felt looking at Della as she stood there in her bathing suit was another thing altogether.

He took in the body-hugging black one-piece suit she wore. It was so… Della. It was like the suits he saw in pictures of fifties and sixties actresses—the bombshells—but it suited Della perfectly. Modest but sexy all at the same time. The material showed every curve and allowed a tempting peek at the cleavage he wanted to get a lot closer to. The walk down from the mountain had been hot in more ways than one, and Gabe wanted to finish what they'd started there.

"My toe doesn't lie," she said, arching a doubtful eyebrow in his direction.

He treaded water, and reached down, shucking his swim trunks and throwing them up on the dock next to her feet. She shrieked and laughed as the cold water splashed her.

"Now, jump in, and I promise I'll keep you warm," he said with a crook of his finger.

She looked around, but no one else was in sight. There was an easy fifty yards of wooded terrain between the cabins and the lake.

Biting her lip, she still looked apprehensive, but closed her eyes and did a graceful dive, breaking the surface with an outraged gasp a few feet away from him.

"It is *so* cold!" she accused, her teeth chattering. "You lie."

Gabe ignored the stab of guilt her accusation caused and closed the space between them, pulling her up against him and wrapping his arms around her. Within seconds, her shivering stopped. He licked kisses along the curve of her neck and shoulder, his erection already rubbing against her hip.

Her eyes widened. "How is *that* even possible in this icy water?"

"It's you, Della…you have me so hot I'm surprised we're not creating steam on the surface. Besides," he said, as he slid one strap of her suit off her shoulder, "it really does warm up after you're in for a few minutes. You just need to keep moving."

"It is getting warmer, I think," she said, reaching under the surface to take him in her hand as they kissed.

Gabe groaned, the playful mood turning to something more urgent as he moved into her touch, but as good as her fingers felt on him, it wasn't enough.

"I want to be inside you, Della, now," he said in her ear. "But we don't have any protection out here. I can promise you I'm healthy, but I understand if you don't want to take my word for it."

The way she looked into his eyes as she slid the other strap of her suit from her shoulder nearly did him in.

"You'll have to take my word for it, too, and I'm using birth control," she said, and finished wiggling out of the rest of her suit until they were naked together under the water.

Gabe took her suit and flung it up on the dock along with his before he brought her legs up around his hips, wrapping her around him as he found his way inside the silky heat of her body.

Home, something in his subconscious seemed to echo, surprising him. That was a feeling, and a word, that he never associated with sex.

"Oh, Gabe, that's so good," she said on a gasp as he filled her completely and stayed there for a moment, the two of them as close as any two humans could possibly be.

He liked Della, and could even admit to caring for her, but now there was an overwhelming need and tenderness that made him stop, catch his breath, find his footing.

Except that he was, literally and figuratively, in over his head, so he moved them a few feet closer to the dock, where he could find a firm stance on the sandy bottom.

"Everything with you feels good, Della." It was true. With her, he felt like a different man. Like he had hope, and was rediscovering things about life he had forgotten about, or given up on.

Claiming her mouth in a hard kiss, need taking over his softer emotions for a moment, he focused on how soft and slick her skin was, cool, still from the water, against his own heat. She didn't seem to mind, sinking her fingers into his hair, returning the kiss as passionately, rolling her hips in the way that drove him insane.

"I love how you do that," he said, closing his eyes.

"What?"

"When you move like that…"

"Like this?" she whispered against his mouth, doing it again.

"Yeah, but keep doing it and this won't last long."

She smiled, her lashes spiked with drops of water, her blue eyes indigo with desire as she held his gaze and did it again. Gabe took her bottom in both hands, controlling her movement so that he did last. As much as she pushed him toward release, he didn't want this to end. Didn't want what was on the other side of this moment, this weekend.

Reality. His leaving. No Della.

The prospect felt bleak, and he dismissed it, returning instead to the heat of her body and how he felt deep inside of her.

Just take this, it's as much as you're ever going to get, and maybe more than you deserve, he thought to himself, starting to move in a way he knew would drive her over the edge.

He was right. Her head tipped back, her fingers digging into the muscles of his arms as she made those sweet, aroused noises that told him she was close. Moments later, his knees nearly gave out under him as she was shuddering through her release, her arms and legs wrapped tightly around him. He followed, the skin-on-skin contact proving too much for him to resist. He couldn't maintain his control against the passion she shared with him.

"Della, you turn me inside out," he mumbled against the curve of her neck, and held her tighter as they cooled down.

"Me, too," she whispered back.

Gabe led her out into deeper depths, where they loosened their hold on each other and swam for a while. He was not surprised to find Della was an able swimmer—better than he was, really.

They both turned when a rumbling sound echoed behind them, to discover that dark clouds had invaded the horizon.

"Storm coming in," he called. "We'd better get out."

"Race you back to the dock?" she offered in return, eager for the challenge.

Gabe was spent, but he couldn't say no, not when she looked like some sexy sea nymph, her curly hair wet around her face, cheeks flushed, smiling.

As they both pushed through the water, back to the dock, where their suits had dried in the sun, he came up several yards short of the win. In fact, she had picked up her suit from the dock and was pulling it back on, mostly under the cover of the lake, when he finally caught up.

Grabbing his shorts and putting them on underwater as well, they climbed the ladder and walked toward the cabin just as a light rain started.

"You're a heck of a swimmer," he commented, chagrined to be slightly out of breath as they made their way quickly up the path as the rain intensified.

"All those years at college with nothing much else to do, I spent a lot of time doing laps in the pool. I still swim a few times a week. I try to run, but I don't like it as much as swimming."

"So that explains the smokin' hot bod," he said with a leer as he wiggled his eyebrows.

She laughed, and still had a hint of a blush around her cheeks.

"Well, at the very least, it keeps me in shape. Doing what I do, I sit at a desk a lot, sit in planes a lot, and so forth. And I like food, so…"

"No complaints here," he said as the rain became heavier and a bolt of lightning flashed over the lake. He quickly fished out the key from where they had hidden it before heading down to the dock.

But underneath the rock, his fingers felt only dirt; he discovered the key several inches back from where he'd left it. Maybe an animal had tried to make off with it?

Or maybe he'd kicked it when he turned away? It was probably nothing, but the hairs on the back of his neck insisted otherwise.

"What's wrong?"

Gabe stood, shaking his head. "Nothing. I just didn't see the key at first, and thought I had the wrong rock."

He opened the door to the cozy cabin and they ducked inside just as the clouds opened, rain pouring down in sheets as thunder and lightning crashed around them.

Gabe peered out the window. "I forgot how storms can come up so quickly in this heat and humidity. Glad we made it back in time, it's pretty fierce out there."

"I love storms, though. And they are so much different here than in the city," she said, standing next to him by the window, taking it all in.

Gabe watched her rather than the storm, envying how she soaked up every experience, took it in whole, and it all came shining out of her eyes, her expression. He'd forgotten, for the most part, how to take such pleasure in simple things, like a thunderstorm, a swim in a lake, or a mountain climb. Della was putting him back in touch with that.

It felt good. It felt like...living again. When Janet had died, had he really given up on life so much? It seemed so. Until now.

His hand had curved around Della's shoulder as they stood taking in the rain, and he stroked the nape of her neck, his thumb sliding under the strap of her suit.

"It doesn't show any sign of letting up soon," he murmured.

She turned toward him, her hand planted on his chest over his heart. "No, I'd say we're probably stuck inside for a while."

He was ready again, wanting more of her, and she knew that, the increased thud of his heart under her hand making her eyes widen slightly as she looked up at him.

"Wow," she whispered.

"That's what you do, Della, every time I'm near you," he said.

She started to say something back, but he took the words away with a kiss, not wanting to talk. Gabe only wanted to feel everything he could, to learn from Della and squeeze everything that was possible from the moment. To live again.

Walking her back from the window, he slid the

straps from her suit down her shoulders, and they both shucked their clothes on their way to the huge bed that dominated one side of the cabin.

To his surprise and delight, Della stopped short of the bed and surprised him by planting a hand on his chest and pushing him firmly back on to it, leaning over him. Her pretty blue eyes sparkled with sexy intent as she crawled up over him and pinned his hands down on either side of his head.

"Now, you stay put and let me show you what I wanted to do to you up on the mountain."

She delivered the command with mock severity, which nonetheless had him more aroused, and definitely intrigued.

Gabe sure wasn't about to argue as she kissed her way down his body and continued to surprise him, rocking his world—she was also changing it more than she knew. Maybe more than both of them knew, he thought, before she took him between her lovely lips and proceeded to wipe away any clear thoughts at all, and Gabe was more than happy to let her.

DELLA WOKE UP alone in the huge, soft bed, naked and disoriented. It took her a second to let her eyes adjust to the dim morning light before her mind cleared and she remembered where she was. The cabin. With Gabe.

A smile stretched across her lips as she recalled everything about the time she and Gabe had spent together here. It was special, and to her, at least, far past anything she could even define as a "fling."

She cared for Gabe. Maybe more than cared. She felt his pain when he told her about his loss, and when he smiled—in the rare moments when he seemed truly carefree and open, like he had in the lake—it moved her deeply. When he made love to her, and told her how she affected him, it made her feel like the center of the universe. No one had ever made her feel that way. Like she was the sun, shining only for him.

There was more than desire, and more than sex between them. At least for her. She couldn't deny that, even knowing he would probably deny it. There were moments when she was sure he was feeling the connection between them as deeply as she did, but then in the next moment, it would be gone. He would be distant again, the mask in place.

All she could really go on were her own feelings, and that was okay. This was, perhaps, the first time she had really started to fall for someone, and it was spectacular. And that he wanted her, too, was more than she had dreamed of.

She wanted to enjoy it, even if it hurt like hell later, when he left. The sharp pain of missing him hit her, even at the thought.

Which made her wonder where he was. The cabin was silent, and there was no sign of him. Snatching up her phone, she saw it was around eight in the morning. The rain hadn't passed completely, making the room darker than it normally would be at this time of the day. A chill grabbed her as she slid out from under the thick blanket.

Della took a robe from the back of a nearby chair and padded to the kitchen, where she saw a white slip of paper on the counter, near a pot of coffee.

Back soon, went to find some breakfast, G.

Della smiled, relieved, and poured a cup of coffee while she waited, stepping out onto the small porch outside the door, taking in the view. The sun was starting to peek through the clouds on the horizon over the lake, and so the day would clear up soon. Her mind relaxed and the stress from her daily existence had completely dissipated. Maybe she should find a retreat like this to visit alone, to work, and to think.

But she only had one more day here with Gabe. Then what?

Back to her life, to setting it all back to rights, the wedding, getting her home fixed and refurnished, preparing for the new semester and her speaking trip to Italy. Her life would move forward, and so would Gabe's. The thought created a small well of sadness in her chest, but she chased it away. She'd known what she was getting into. She'd get over it, and all of this would be a happy memory. Eventually, there would be someone else.

She tried to picture it, and couldn't. The only face that appeared in her mind's eye, and in her heart, was Gabe's.

Then she saw him, walking up the path with two bags, and her mood brightened immediately.

"Morning," she said, smiling as he approached.

He looked completely different than he did in the city. No suit, for one thing, just jeans, boots and a black T-shirt that molded over every muscle.

He smiled back. "Hey. I woke up starving, and what we had on hand to eat wasn't going to cut it after all that exercise, so I went down to the camp store for a few more things while you were sleeping."

"Thank you, oh…what smells so good in there?" she asked as he came closer, the scents of cinnamon and spice rising up through the cool, damp morning air.

"They make their own doughnuts. I showed up just as they had a new batch coming out. Got some bacon and eggs, too."

Della followed him inside where they both scarfed down doughnuts as bacon cooked on the stove.

"Oh, these are so good," she moaned, licking some cinnamon and sugar from her fingertips and then smiling as she noticed Gabe watching her just as hungrily.

"You go get dressed, and I'll finish up the bacon and eggs. The weather will clear soon, and maybe we can go down into town and walk around."

"Sounds perfect," she said, leaning over to offer a kiss.

Then another, and another, until Gabe laughed, pushing her away.

"Go, before the bacon burns… I need the protein to keep up with you, vixen."

Della conceded, but only because she was so pleased at being called a vixen. Smiling all the way to the shower, she emerged to the delicious aromas of breakfast and agreed that the doughnuts, delectable as they were, weren't enough to sustain her.

As she passed through the hall, she knocked her bag from the table where she'd left it, and the contents spilled everywhere. She quickly righted it, picking up the mess, though as she did so, she noticed a small metallic item on the floor that didn't look like anything of hers.

Picking it up, she looked at it more closely, and while she couldn't say exactly, dread seeped down through her body, smothering any joy and warmth that had been there before. Hands shaking, she fought the urge to throw the small disk from her hands, and ran out to Gabe instead.

"Gabe, is this what I think it is? I found it in my bag," she asked, her voice shaking.

He stood at the counter, his smile at seeing her fading as he realized something was wrong.

She held out her hand as he crossed to inspect what she had, his expression darkening, posture becoming stiff.

"It's a tracker, isn't it? I've only seen a few, some of the tech guys at school were working on a project with GPS chips so small they could barely be detected, but that's what it is, isn't it?"

"Yes, that's what it is."

Panic had her rushing back to the bathroom, where her cases were.

"We need to pack—we need to get out of here. Someone knows I'm here, someone is following me... us," she blurted, suddenly terrified. "It has to be whoever was in my home, and whoever was following me. I knew someone was following me. I *knew* it, but why?"

"Della. Della," Gabe said, more loudly the second time. "Stop. Please."

He'd followed her into the bathroom, and Della fought for calm as he took the chip from her fingers and stared at it, his jaw tight, not saying a word.

"Gabe?"

Her shoulders squared, tensed. He had what she had come to think of as "that look"—the one when the mask slid over his features and the real Gabe, the one she knew when he was alone with her, disappeared.

"Della, we have to talk."

She crossed her arms in front of her, a chill running down her spine.

"You're scaring me."

He stepped in, put a hand on her shoulder. "I don't mean to. C'mon, let's get some food and I'll…explain this."

Her mind sharpened and she turned out of his touch.

"Explain that? You mean, you *know* about that?"

He sighed, understanding that she wasn't going anywhere, that she wasn't going to be cowed or managed until he told her what was going on.

"I know about it because…it's mine. I put it in your bag, and another in your coat, after the incident at your office."

Della's mind scrambled to catch up.

"Wait…why? Why would you do that?"

"Can we go in the other room and sit, please? This might take a little while."

She wanted to say no, but she nodded instead. This was Gabe, and he had to have an explanation, right? She turned, went into the main room of the cabin and sat. She waited while he poured coffee and brought her some food, though she ignored it. She couldn't even think about putting something in her stomach right now.

Gabe sat across from her in a chair, not next to her. Not close. Facing her. Adversarial. But his tone was soft, his expression hesitant.

"The case I was working…it involved a project you were associated with some months ago, with Arch Labs. Do you remember?"

"Sure. I did risk analysis for them on a vaccine project, though I wasn't told many details."

He nodded. "Okay, I'm going to fill you in—and tell you more than you're cleared to know, but it's time. And Della, you need to know, before I get into the meat of it, that what has happened between us, me and you… this has meant something to me. You have to understand that. I'm telling you everything because I want you to know… I owe you at least that."

Della fought the urge to curl her legs up, to pull herself into a protective posture in the face of his vague statements that nonetheless were making her blood run cold, the dull weight of dread in her stomach.

"Our meeting, on the plane, wasn't an accident…" he began, and to her silent, stunned amazement, continued to tell her about how he switched their bags on purpose, had been running a check on her in connection to his case and had needed to clear her of any suspicion of being involved with the theft of the information at the lab.

"So you thought I could be involved in the data breach at the labs?"

"Not just you, we investigated everyone connected to the project, and you were not our main suspect by any means. In fact, you were highly tangential, and I cleared you almost immediately."

"So why were you following me?"

Della's mind was frozen by the shock of what she was hearing—Gabe had been the one following her? The night of the cooking class, he'd already known where she was, and even before that? He knew she was worried, thinking she was being paranoid, and he let her think that?

"I know you had nothing to do with it, not willingly, anyway," he added. "But the interviews with the lab staff weren't revealing anything, and when you were chased at your office, and your home was invaded, we had to refocus on you. In fact, the break-in at your home coincided with the move we made to close down the project at the lab and move the entire thing to a secure military site."

"I don't understand—why would those two things connect?"

"When we discovered that Cedric Derian was involved—and that he targets academics, in particular—we suspected that he was either trying to cover his tracks or make a last-minute play to still get the data, or to find out where it went. At that point, I couldn't afford to take my eyes off of you. Cedric is known for... well, not leaving any loose ends behind."

Della shook her head. "So you, this…coming here… you were protecting me?"

"In part, mostly, yes."

"What does that mean, 'in part'?"

He took a deep breath. "The mission changed. If Derian is cleaning up his operation, that means you're in danger, which means he'll come after you."

"So, what you really mean is that you still aren't sure if I was involved, and so you were following me to see if I would lead you to them, as well as trying to protect me from them? I'm bait?"

"No, yes… I mean, I'm fairly sure that you aren't directly involved—"

"Fairly sure? Let me assure you, I am *not* involved. I don't know this person, and I have had no contact with anyone regarding the lab work I did at all."

Now the chill between them laced her words, her posture.

"I believe you. But that doesn't mean that they aren't using you in some way, without your knowledge. And that puts you in even more danger."

Della considered, trying to sort it all out, and most especially pushing down the raging hurt that was threatening to take over everything rational.

"So sleeping with me, all of this," she said, waving her hand around the cabin, "was just to stay close, to find out if I was involved or if I would lead you to your target?"

She was proud of herself for being able to say the words aloud without choking on the bitter emotion that festered beneath them. But he stood suddenly from the chair, crossing to sit beside her now, making her pull back reflexively.

"No. I mean, at the start, yes. But… I wanted to see you, and until I found out about Cedric, it was just…us. It's still just us, here. It's two separate things."

"Except that you are tracking me, and also thinking some deranged terrorist is after me. Other than that, it's just us?" she asked, pain and disbelief fueling her sarcasm. "It's not separate at all, at least not for me."

"I know, it's complicated."

She huffed a humorless laugh. He reached for her hand, and she pulled it back.

"The next thing you'll tell me is that I don't even know your real name, right?"

She was making a harsh joke, but when she saw him draw himself in, his face closing down, she knew the truth.

"I don't," she whispered more to herself than him. "I've been sleeping with you, and sharing everything about myself—more than I have with anyone… You know *everything* about me, and I don't even know your real name."

She stood now, needing to get as much distance as she could from Gabe…or whoever he was.

"I'm sorry, Della. I never expected this…you. I care for you, and what I feel for you is real, but I also have to keep you safe. Do my job. It's a mess, I know. I haven't wanted to lie to you, and I didn't want to involve you in this."

The pained look on his face at her withdrawing from him, the tone of his voice, so sincere, almost moved her, but how could she trust any of it?

"So, what is your real name, then? If you told me the rest of this, can you tell me that, at least?"

He hesitated, and she closed her eyes, taking a breath.

"I see."

"I can't, Della. Not yet."

"Yet? What does that mean? Were you planning to? I thought you were leaving?"

Some small hope leaped in her heart, that maybe he wasn't leaving, maybe he would stay, and then…

"I don't know. I don't know what I was planning to do, except close the case, keep you safe. I don't know what I was going to do then, except that I…"

She held her breath, waiting.

"I've felt more alive with you than I have in a long time. I hadn't even realized it, until now, and I hated the lies, and the things I had to do—"

"But you still do them, even now."

He nodded. "Until this is done, yes. Like I said, until you're safe."

She wanted to believe him, but how could she know

he wasn't still playing her? That he had to keep her on the hook to close his case? Of course he did.

"You could have simply asked me. Interviewed me. I don't know too many people, not close friends, and what does this Derian look like? I could tell you if I know him."

"He changes his face, his look. Even his accent, his voice. We have very few pictures, fewer leads because he doesn't leave a trace behind. Don't you see? That's why we're here, why I have to do this," he said, pointing to the tracker. "Because if he is involved, if you are, then he won't walk away until he's dealt with you. Even if you don't know him, have never set eyes on him, he—"

"He'll kill me."

Gabe nodded. "Or have you killed. And I think we've pushed him now. Whoever he's getting this information for, they're not going to like it if he comes up empty-handed, so he's desperate, too. Maybe desperate enough to do something stupid."

"And that's how you can catch him."

"I hope so. But if it involves you, which I believe it does, then I have to keep you close. I'll protect you."

"So…why this weekend here?"

He closed his eyes, took a deep breath. "I wanted time with you, away from it."

"Or, if he is the one after me, you could lure him out more easily here."

"It was a possibility. But I won't let him hurt you."

"And what if you're completely wrong? What if he's not after me and I'm not involved at all? Then this has been a waste of time?"

His time with her, she meant, and she couldn't keep her voice from cracking on the final note.

He closed the space between them, looking fierce. She tried to move back, but he didn't let her, his hands closing over her upper arms, making her stay, making her look at him.

"I know it's bad, Della, and I know I've lied to you, but not about everything. When it was just us, it wasn't a lie. The things I told you, about Janet, and my family, that was all true."

She wanted to believe him, but she honestly didn't know what to believe at the moment. He'd used her, in more ways than one, regardless of the motive—to catch a terrorist, to keep her safe. Did that make it better?

Too many conflicting emotions crowded the field, and Della just wasn't equipped to deal with them. So she shoved them aside, burying them under a more rational approach to the problem.

"You need to find this guy, and you think he's going to come after me for some reason?"

"Yes."

"Okay," she said simply, turning out of his hold and moving back to the bath, where she picked up her things and started repacking her bag.

He followed, clearly unsure. "Della?"

She took a deep breath, shut off the confusion, focusing on what was most important.

"You have a job to do, and I've become part of that, whether I like it or not. How long will you be following me? How long will this last?"

"I have until the end of the week."

One week. She could get through that. She turned to face him, drawing herself up straight.

"Okay. You do what you need to, I'll help. But this… this thing between us, it's over. Tell me what you need me to do, and I'll do it, but I won't sleep with you. That's it."

He regarded her quietly for a few minutes, and then nodded.

"Okay. Thank you."

When he turned and left, walking out to get ready to leave as well, Della couldn't help the sharp pain from taking over. He'd accepted her terms so easily, so calmly. No objections whatsoever.

She curled over her bag as she finished packing. Hot, heavy tears fell on the blue canvas of the suitcase as she zipped it, and as she did so, she tried to do the same to her emotions.

There'd be time for that later. Time to lick her wounds in private and move on, but for the moment, she wouldn't let him see how much he'd hurt her. That was her fault, anyway. She shouldn't have fallen for him. But she had—or rather, she'd fallen for the lie.

It was a mistake, she reassured herself, that she'd never make again.

11

GABE TUGGED AT the tie he wore as he sat on one of the hard wooden benches that were set up in rows on either side of the aisle in the garden where Chloe and Justin's wedding would be taking place the next day.

But neither the tie, nor the heat, nor the bench was the real source of his discomfort. That was settled squarely in his gut—and as crass as it was to say so, a few inches lower, as well. It had been almost a week since he returned from the mountains with Della. A week of clipped conversations when they were on their own, and worse, faked conversations—at least on her part—when they were with others. For most of the week, she made a concerted effort not to be alone with him whenever possible.

True to his word, he'd shadowed her everywhere, from picking up flowers, to checking on the cake delivery and even sitting in the background—unbeknownst to anyone but Della—watching. Even when he was with her, at the bachelorette party, he felt like an outsider.

That had been particularly tough, especially when

the fun and games included everyone sharing a sexy story over their dessert. The one Della shared—with dramatic relish, no doubt for his effect—was not about him. That had stung.

He couldn't blame her, but…with nothing happening during the week, and Bart almost to the point of ordering him back to D.C. or telling him to quit, Gabe was almost seriously entertaining the latter option. In fact, he was only here now because he couldn't quite walk away yet.

Clearly, his instincts were off. Nothing had occurred since their return, Della's apartment was almost back to normal, and she seemed perfectly safe. There had been no further incidents, and it was as if his gut instincts were wrong.

He'd let other emotions entirely take over his thinking, clouding his judgment, no doubt leading him in wrong directions. He cared for Della, and it weighed heavier as the days went on, knowing he hurt her, knowing that she hated him and knowing that it had all been for nothing made it even worse.

He shook his head in disgust at his own thoughts. He'd never been one for so much naval-gazing. He was a guy who liked action, but what exactly did he want to do? Go back to D.C. and dive into another mission, or stay here, and try to win Della back?

Was that even possible?

He wasn't fit for duty, and he wasn't fit for Della, either. She deserved better.

Glowering, he looked behind him, wondering what the heck was going on. How long did it take to practice walking down a path and reciting some vows, anyway?

Finally, Justin appeared at the front near the podium that had been set up, with another man beside him.

Gabe focused on the best man, something triggering in his mind. He looked familiar. Pulling out his phone, he pulled up the most recent picture of Derian, but he quickly saw that there was no resemblance, not even a buried one.

As someone gave instructions from the side, Gabe couldn't help the niggling feeling of familiarity, though, as he looked at the guy. Until some music started, and he saw Della start her march down the aisle.

She was dressed in normal clothes, like the rest of them, measuring her steps and avoiding meeting his eyes at all costs.

Gabe, on the other hand, didn't take his eyes from her. In fact, as he watched her walk by, it was all he could do not to reach out and touch.

He missed her. He missed their conversations, her humor, openness and passion. He missed her body next to his and her smile, which was reserved for others now.

Would he be able to walk away and forget her? He'd done it before with other women, but Della wasn't just another woman.

Chloe took her cue now, almost floating down the aisle with her graceful stature, like that of a model, her smile and eyes directly on the groom.

Gabe fantasized, suddenly, about Della looking at him that way. About Della coming down the aisle to meet him and them spending the rest of their lives together.

His chest tightened until he almost couldn't breathe,

and he was only able to change that by admitting it was what he wanted. Della, with him, for good. For real.

He'd done a lot of seemingly impossible tasks in the course of his job, and among them, he'd convinced a lot of people to do things they wouldn't normally do. Certainly, he could convince her, in time, to forgive him, couldn't he?

He'd start by calling Bart on Monday and making official his decision about the job. He wouldn't be going back. There would be no next mission.

He wanted to interrupt the proceedings, to tell Della what he wanted and what he planned to do, but he sat and watched quietly, waiting for the right moment.

He needed a strategy. This was a delicate operation.

Gabe didn't even hear the rest of the ceremony going on around him as he formulated a plan, a strategy to convince Della to give him a second chance.

It started of course, with telling her his real name.

But not tonight; not until after the wedding. She had enough going on, and he didn't want to appear to be taking advantage of her. Until then, he had to be patient, to stay by her side and fine-tune his approach.

His final mission, he thought with a small smile.

Glancing up, he caught Della watching him, somewhat curiously, before she grimaced and averted her gaze. Gabe's resolve strengthened. He would melt the icy distance between them if it was the last thing he ever did.

Content to sit contemplating his plan while the activities went on around him, Gabe didn't see Della walk up, standing a few feet away as she only met his eyes fleetingly.

"What are you up to?" she asked suspiciously, her beautiful smile forced and strained.

"I'm just sitting here, as instructed."

"Something is up. I could tell by your expression, how you were looking at me."

He almost smiled. She could read him. Normally, for an undercover agent, that wasn't a good thing; but with Della, it pleased him that she knew him so well. Even now, when she was so angry with him.

"I'll tell you later. Is this over? What do we do now?"

She sighed, frowning more deeply. "We have to go to dinner."

"You sound like you would rather eat tacks."

Her shoulders dropped and she sat in the chair one seat away from him. "I need this—all of this—to be over. The wedding is stressful enough, but having you watch every move I make… I can't sleep. My focus is off. I keep expecting something to happen, but nothing has. Obviously, you were wrong about this whole thing. It has nothing to do with me. And you're being here just makes it…more difficult."

Guilt panged in Gabe's chest, and he leaned in, closing some of the space she kept putting between them.

"I'm sorry. It's not easy for me, either, believe me, watching you and not being able to…be with you."

Her eyes widened, color infusing her cheeks. "I don't even want to talk about that."

"Are you sure?" he asked, taking her hand in his.

It wasn't playing nice, breaking the rules and touching her like that, but Gabe wasn't necessarily going to play nice to get through her defenses. She tugged away from his grasp as he rubbed his thumb over her knuckles. The pulse in her throat sped visibly, and his heartbeat picked up as her lips parted, as if to catch her breath. It was all he could do not to take advantage and steal a taste.

"Relax, Della. You're doing fine."

"Why are you doing this?" she whispered, an edge of desperation in her voice. "You know we're not—"

"Because I miss you," he said simply, truthfully.

Her reply was cut short by the announcement that they were all heading to the restaurant for dinner. Gabe stood, sliding his arm around Della's shoulders as they walked out. She stiffened beneath his touch.

"Hey, this is supposed to be fun, remember?" He dropped a kiss on the top of her head, inhaling the scent of her hair.

She glared, pulling away as she crossed the lot to the car he'd rented for the wedding.

"She doesn't look pleased."

Gabe turned to see Justin standing beside him, and nodded.

"I guess all couples argue sooner or later," he said. "She's been under a lot of stress."

"I know. Chloe and I appreciate everything she's done for the wedding, but we may have asked too much. We have something special planned for her as a thank-you."

"She'll appreciate that, I'm sure. Good luck to you as well," Gabe offered with a handshake and a smile.

"Thanks," Justin replied, turning back to the door as Chloe emerged.

Gabe joined a seething Della in the rental car. She didn't say a word as they followed the others to the rehearsal dinner venue.

"Della, it's going to be okay," he said softly, his hand on her arm as she tried to bolt from the car as soon as he shut the engine off.

She stilled under his touch. "I'm fine."

"You're not. Neither am I."

"What do you mean?"

Gabe got out, crossing around the car to open her door, helping her out, standing close.

"I'm not okay without you," he said.

Her eyes filled. "I wish you wouldn't say things like that to me."

He groaned, pulling her in close. "I know things are bad right now, but for the moment, let's just pretend nothing changed. We can enjoy the evening, okay? I told Justin we had an argument, but maybe it's time we made up?"

"You're right, I'm being selfish. I don't want to ruin this for them."

"You're not doing that. You've done a terrific job, and you deserve to enjoy all of your efforts, as well." He looked down into her face. "And listen, you're right. The investigation is a bust, and you have no reason to be worried or afraid. So let's try to have some fun tonight, okay? Put the rest behind us?"

She nodded and looked away. "I'm not as good at faking it as you are."

"Then don't," he said simply, cupping his palm around her elbow and heading to the entrance of the restaurant. "Just be yourself. And for the record, I'm not faking how I feel about you, honey."

She seemed surprised, but still wary, as they walked into the restaurant and on to a private room, where their party was set up. Each table was decorated simply with pretty white flowers in crystal vases, and a bottle of champagne and glasses for toasting. A dance floor was in the center of the room, with a small stage for a band that was also starting to organize themselves.

"I thought a rehearsal dinner was only for the bridal party?" he asked, seeing more people streaming in.

"Well, there are only four of us, and Chloe likes a party, so she opened it up to all of their friends."

Gabe nodded. "Go do what you need to, and I'll be right here," he said, offering her a slight kiss on the cheek. He then found his way to the bar on the other side of the room.

At least she didn't glare or shy away from him that time. Maybe there was hope.

Della crossed the room to talk to the restaurant manager as more guests arrived, glancing back with a mix of confusion and what Gabe hoped was something softer and more positive. It wasn't easy to hold back, not when he wanted to just blurt everything out and let her know how he felt. He intended to make everything up to her, starting by helping her to enjoy this evening. After that, he suspected things were going to get a lot more complicated, but he was determined to get through to Della, one way or another.

THE CHAMPAGNE WAS EXCELLENT, and after everyone was seated, her toast delivered and dinner served, Della took full advantage of the bottle at her table.

"They look happy," Gabe commented as he refilled her glass, and then his own.

She looked at Chloe and Justin, and agreed. They were happy. Truly in love, best friends. They didn't lie to each other or use each other for their own ends.

Her eyes stung—as if she hadn't cried enough already that week—and she hastily took a sip of her wine to choke back the tears.

"Della, honey—" Gabe's voice was soft, and she turned her face away, knowing he'd seen.

"Don't call me that, please," she said, practically begging.

Didn't he understand how hard it was for her? That she was more than halfway to falling in love with him—which was her fault, and she could have dealt with it. Except that everything had been a lie. He'd lied to her from the start, and even his endearments, his soft words to her now, were lies. How could she ever trust herself or her feelings, her judgment? Nothing in her life had prepared her for this.

Thinking about it made her angry again, but at least anger was easier.

"You said I'm not in danger, as you thought, so why are you even here?" she asked, turning on him.

The others at their table were up dancing, so they were alone, and no one else would hear over the music.

He frowned and said, "C'mon, let's dance."

"I don't want—"

But apparently she had no choice in the matter, as his hand caught hers and pulled her along with him. She tried to put some space between them, to not stand with her body so flush against his, but he held her firm.

She resented it, and she wanted it…he felt so good, it was almost torture.

What was wrong with her that she wanted him so much, still, in spite of everything that happened? When he touched her, or said something sweet, even when it was a lie, she still wanted it.

That fact made her ashamed of herself, but not so much that she didn't give in and sink against him. They moved in a natural rhythm that their bodies seemed to find almost automatically.

"Della, we need to talk, tonight," he said against her ear, making a shiver run down her spine.

Her head swam slightly—too much champagne, not enough sleep or food, and she held on tighter.

"No—no more talking," she replied, tired to the bone. Tired of resisting, hurting and feeling so awful.

No doubt what Gabe wanted to tell her was that he was heading home. Maybe he'd come here tonight to make up for some of his lies, and she supposed that was something. He could have just left her high and dry without a date.

It didn't even matter at this point. Warmed by his body for the first time this week, her anger dissolved, her need taking over as she gave in to the impulse to curl in and let him tell her whatever lies he wanted to for one more night. Then he could go.

It would hurt afterward, but no more than it had hurt all week since she'd found the tracker in her bag.

When she was this close to him, she could lie to herself, and bury the hurt underneath desire. Running her hands over the expanse of his back and seeing the pulse in his throat pick up pace, she smiled. Forgetting was exactly what she wanted right now, and she knew Gabe could make that happen.

"Della…" He started to object as she slid a hand up to pull him down to her, kissing him so he wouldn't say anything else.

She didn't want to know what he was going to say, she only wanted to feel something good.

She pressed against him, reveled in how hard he was—so at least he *was* telling the truth about missing her.

"Della, no," he said, stepping back slightly.

That stung.

"Wait. *Now* you're unwilling to have sex with me, when I know the truth? Could you only do it while you were lying to me? Don't worry, I still don't know who you are, and I won't come looking for you later," she spat at him, turning away before her tears betrayed her.

She didn't care who heard, though the music was so loud no one seemed to notice. Turning away, she rushed to the door, needing to get out. Her duties for the night were done, no one needed her—especially not Gabe.

GABE CAUGHT UP in the parking lot, turned her back into his arms. She wrenched away, but he didn't let her and then he saw her face, stained with tears, her features deeply etched with hurt.

"I'm sorry, Della, I… You know I want you. You have to know that," he said.

But undoing what he'd done wasn't that easy.

"Let me go."

"I don't want to let you go."

"Really? So why push me away? What are these mind games, Gabe? Why are you doing this?"

He wiped tears from her face with his thumb, surprised at how much it pained him to see her cry. Especially when he was the cause.

"It's not mind games. It's me trying to do the right thing. I do want you, but we need to talk."

She shook her head. "I don't want to talk. There's too much spinning around in my head already. I want to feel something good right now. That's all. That's all I was asking for. If you can't do that, then leave."

Gabe took a breath, realizing that he needed to come clean, to put everything right, to ease his own conscience. To tell her how he felt, so that *he* could feel better.

But what if she didn't want that? What if he was too late, and all she wanted from him was, as she said, to feel good? Maybe the best thing for Della wasn't *him*.

Suddenly, looking at her, he doubted that he could fix this, that he'd hurt her too much—and maybe all he could offer her was all they'd ever had. His heart sank, but he pushed that aside. Right now, this was about Della, and what she needed. Putting his needs aside, he focused on that, on giving her what she wanted.

"Okay, yes, I can do that," he said, pulling her in against him, moving his hands over her neck and her back until she relaxed and softened into him. "I can definitely make you feel good."

She nodded against his chest, and he lifted her face, glad to see the tears gone, and desire had replaced the sadness that was there before.

Her lips were salty from crying, though, a reminder of the damage he'd done, and while arousal gripped him, he slowed down, trying to undo some of it. The thought made him gentle, stroking her back and her arms, kissing her until she was leaning into him as if unable to stand.

"This is a good start," she said against his throat, and he chuckled.

"Let's go," he whispered in her ear as people emerged from the restaurant behind them and he led her to the car.

But before he could start the engine, she was leaning

against him, her hands everywhere, her tongue leaving hot little licks along his neck, under his ear.

"Della—"

"Just drive, Gabe."

He knew she was using him to block out her pain, and that was the motivation for her aggressiveness, but he found it extremely erotic nonetheless. His body hardened under her insistent kisses and how she pressed her palm against him made it difficult to think straight, or focus on the city traffic, which thankfully lightened up as they made their way back to her apartment.

By the time he pulled into the parking space down the street, Gabe wasn't sure he could get out of the car and walk the distance to the door without embarrassing himself. One look at Della, her hair mussed, lips swollen from kissing, and he didn't care what anyone else thought.

Stepping out of the car, he took her hand and they hurried toward the building. But before they reached it, he pulled her close, turning the tables. She'd nearly driven him mad on the journey over here, and now it was his turn. Maybe she was right—this was good, and it was nice to forget, for a few minutes, anyway.

"I missed you, Della," he said raggedly as he closed his hands over her breasts, loving how she arched into his touch.

"No talking," she said, panting out the words as her nipples budded against his palms.

"Oh, I'm going to talk. I'm going to tell you everything I want to do to you, and then I'm going to do it," he said, leaning in to whisper raw, unadorned words in her ear between kisses.

She didn't object, as they hurried to her door.

"Keys," Gabe demanded.

She already had them in her hand, opened the door and they crowded inside, not bothering to turn on the lights.

That was fine with him—he was happy to feel his way, and his hands and lips knew Della like a blind man knew his own territory.

That didn't mean there weren't new things to explore.

Like the arch of her foot—he had never spent enough time there, he thought, as he took off her shoe and worked his thumbs over that soft spot, enjoying her sigh.

Or the deep cleft behind her knee. He'd sadly ignored that sensitive area, but addressed it thoroughly now with hot, open kisses that made her moan and gasp as he worked his way up her thigh.

"Oh, Gabe, please," she cried out as he found the slick, aroused spot between her thighs that he teased with his tongue, only giving her enough to hold her on the edge.

"Nicholas," he whispered against her skin.

"What?"

"My name is Nicholas," he said. "Nick, if you want."

If it was their last night together, which it might well be, he wanted to hear his real name on her lips.

"Nicholas," she said softly, then again, and as she did so, it was like a barrier had dissolved between them, something giving way. She lay back on the wide bed, opening to him, giving herself freely, and Gabe—Nick—happily seized on the offer.

It felt good to hear her say his real name, and reminded him of how long it had been. To the point where sometimes he forgot to think of himself, his own name, as if *he* didn't really exist. That had always been the case, for his own safety and that of his family—Bart wasn't his boss's real name, either, and Nick didn't know his real one. None of them did. But now…hearing it on Della's lips was one more step back into reality.

It changed everything. Gabe manipulated people, did his job, kept himself separate—always held back. But Nick…he wanted to give Della everything, to get so close that there was nothing between them, not even the breath it took to speak a name.

She didn't want to talk, but actions always spoke louder than words anyway, right?

Gabe used words to deflect, to control. Nick didn't say a word as he lifted up, pulled himself over her and looked down into her face, illuminated only by a sliver of light coming in through the curtains.

Pushing to his back, he brought her up, his hands framing her face as she splayed over him. He was hers, regardless of what happened after this, and his tender kiss sent the message that she could do what she wanted with him. Anything she wanted.

She quivered against him, seeming to understand as she pushed up over his chest, adjusting her seat so that she could take him in, which made him shudder.

No more words as she began to move—this was how they spoke to each other best, anyway. She sighed and fell forward, as if she didn't want any distance between them. Nick reached down, covering her bottom with his hands, stroking and squeezing gently, but not controlling. There had been enough of that, and it felt good to let it go.

Her hands gripped his shoulders as she moved

against him, seeking his mouth, mating her tongue with his as they both approached the point of no return. He swallowed her soft moans and sighs as she tightened around him, pulled him along in the current. He broke the kiss as he caught his breath at the power of his own release, saying her name, repeating it in a chant until the sensation ebbed.

He was grateful that she didn't move away, didn't leave him after the moment passed. Instead, she buried her face in his shoulder, resting her head there, her lips by his ear.

"Nick. I like that. It suits you better," she said, and that was all.

He didn't respond, but rubbed her back until her breathing evened. He stayed awake, wanting to soak up every minute. When she woke again, he was there, ready, and this time, he did take control, squeezing every last ounce of pleasure from them both, as if to store it up for the lonely time ahead.

As they fell asleep again near morning—this time, Nick couldn't fight it—he thought he heard her say something, but his mind lost the words, only hearing her softly mumble, "Maybe we…"

Maybe we…what? All the possibilities the words contained followed him into his dreams.

12

DELLA WAS EXHAUSTED, and relieved. And anxious. And…hopeful, as she examined herself in the mirror in the ladies' room. The wedding had been a beautiful event, and the reception was in full swing. She'd done it, though she wasn't as excited as she should have been.

Her experience with Nick eclipsed all of it. All she had been able to think was that Nick was there, watching her. Every time their eyes met, she relived every single moment of the night before.

Not Gabe, but Nick.

It seemed impossible to think that so much relied on knowing his real name, but the mood between them had definitely changed when he told her. It had been tangible, as if he had shifted bodies or something, finally relaxing, relenting and becoming someone she could connect with in a way that was about more than sex.

Still, he hadn't told her his last name. That worried her. He was one step closer to her, but still kept something back.

Still, she couldn't deny how amazing the night before had been, and not just the sex. Their joining had been more intimate, more…sharing. As if he was trying to tell her something without telling her.

She closed her bag, taking in her reflection and turning to walk out, when Chloe entered, looking as brilliant as she had all day. Della spotted the case in her hand and smiled.

"Getting ready to leave and head off on the honeymoon?"

Chloe smiled. "And then some. It was such a great day, thank you for everything, but I am so ready for the beach."

Della smiled. "Let me help you change, as my last maid-of-honor duty."

"Thank you, I was going to ask. Not sure that I can get out of this monster dress on my own," Chloe said with a laugh, but it didn't seem to reach her eyes.

"Are you okay?" Della asked, picking up on a strange vibe.

"Absolutely! Just tired," Chloe answered, making her way back to the larger dressing room, where she could change.

As Della helped her undo the many small buttons on the back of the dress, Chloe glanced over her shoulder.

"That dress was exactly the right choice. It looks stunning on you, and Gabe seems to agree," she commented. "He hasn't taken his eyes off you all day. I guess you kissed and made up? Justin said you had an argument."

Della smiled. "We did, and I'm glad. I'm sorry if I was in something of a bad mood yesterday."

"I didn't even notice, but I am glad you two are making a go of it."

"Well, I don't know about that, but we'll see what happens," she said, sounding lighter and calmer than she felt.

Then, unexpectedly, Della's cool dissolved as she undid the final button on Chloe's dress. She couldn't hold back hot tears that sprung from her eyes, unbidden.

"Oh, I'm so sorry," she said, stepping away from her friend to find some tissues.

"Della, what's wrong?"

Chloe shucked the dress, wearing only her slip, and crossed the room to put a hand on Della's shoulder.

"I don't know why I'm crying, I mean, I do, but… I'm so sorry, I know this is completely selfish, and not the right time."

Chloe's brow scrunched in concern. "I'm your friend. Tell me."

Della sat on the small bench next to Chloe, and told her everything. That she was in love with Gabe—whose real name was Nick—but that he was DHS undercover, and that he was looking for terrorists who had tried to steal data from a project she was involved in.

"He thought I might be in danger, but clearly that wasn't the case, so I think he'll still be leaving soon. He didn't give me his last name. Technically, he's undercover, and I want to be with him, but I just don't think I can live with this. All the secrets. But I also don't think I can live without him. Not happily," she said miserably, but the tears had stopped.

Apparently, she had needed to say it all out loud, to share what had been eating her up inside for weeks.

"That does explain a lot," Chloe said gently as she stood and crossed the room, reaching into her bag to grab a dress that she slid over her slip, and a pair of black flats, with it. "So he thinks this terrorist is someone you know?"

"That was the theory, but clearly he was wrong."

Chloe folded her dress slowly, and picked up her phone, smiling as she typed something in.

"Sorry. Justin was wondering where I was."

"You guys are so great together," Della offered with a smile as Chloe put her wedding dress in the large bag and zipped it shut.

"I know. He's waiting out by the entrance with Gabe—or rather, Nick—and so maybe we should go out to meet them," Chloe suggested, picking up her things. "Don't worry about Nick—I doubt he's going anywhere. I can almost promise you that."

"How can you know?"

Chloe chuckled. "Married-lady wisdom, I guess. I just don't see him leaving your side."

Della couldn't agree, but hugged her friend and put on her game face as they left the dressing room to meet Justin and Nick.

But when they got to the entrance, the men weren't there.

"Oh, okay," Chloe said, checking her phone again. She nudged Della to turn around. "Go that way. We parked out back when we came in earlier."

Della began walking toward the rear exit.

As they spotted the guys, Della paused for a moment. Something was off in Nick's posture, and he was standing between Justin and his best man—they all seemed too serious.

As they got closer, Della searched their faces. "Is everything okay? You look so—"

"Please, just shut up," Justin spat, rolling his eyes. "I've been listening to you prattle on for months, so right now, just be quiet, please."

Della blinked.

Nick glared at him. "Watch yourself."

Della gasped and lurched back as Justin delivered a punch to Nick's middle, causing him to double over. "Justin!" Della froze then, as she felt something hard pressing into her back.

"Do what he said. Be quiet." Chloe's voice was hard and insistent. She sounded like an entirely different person.

Nick had straightened and Della focused on him, but his expression betrayed nothing. Something was very clearly wrong, but her shock was such that her thoughts were having a tough time catching up, especially to the fact that her good friend apparently had a gun pressed into her spine. "I don't understand," she said softly.

Justin stepped forward, his eyes like flint, wandering over her. "You do look good in that dress, though, I'll give you that. Maybe we'll get to see you out of it before we kill you, hmm?"

"Hey," Chloe objected with a pout, to which Justin, who clearly wasn't Justin, smiled widely and crossed to give her a hard kiss.

"Sorry, love—habit. But maybe I can give her to Pieter to play with."

Nick stepped forward, and the other man, Justin's best man, pulled him back, delivering another punch.

"You must be Pieter," Nick managed, looking up at the man, who just grinned at him, saying nothing.

Della spun on Justin, her heart slamming as she tried to catch her breath and stem her panic.

"What do you want? Who are you?"

"Nick here knows who I am, he just didn't connect the dots until about twenty minutes ago. The plastic surgeons you have here in New York, they truly are the best."

"You're Derian," she whispered.

He laughed, and traced his finger along the low neckline of her dress.

She swatted his hand away; he caught her hand and rewarded her with a slap that stung tears into her eyes.

"Don't touch her!" Nick growled, struggling with the man who was holding him back.

Della crossed toward Chloe—or whoever she was—and took in the gun pointed at her.

"How could you...why?" It was all she could manage.

Chloe stated simply, "Cedric is my life. There's nothing I wouldn't do for him. Nothing at all," she said with a mocking glance.

Della scanned the area, searching for help, for anyone who might see them, but they were completely isolated and alone in the back lot.

There were three of them against her and Nick, and she hardly counted. Apart from some basic self-defense she'd learned in a night class once, she had no idea how to deal with a situation like this.

And yet, she was still desperate for answers.

"Why me, though? What could you possibly want from me?"

"Your risk analysis was critical information for weaponizing the vaccine. But it took time to find it, and download it from your records. Then, that became the perfect back door into the lab, using your credentials, of course."

"All this time?" She looked at Chloe in disbelief.

"No, not at first. Cedric and I met before I met you, and he told me what he needed, and why. I was happy to help. We knew he couldn't approach you directly— you were nowhere near woman enough to handle a man like him," she said with a disparaging look.

Justin laughed. "Yes, and you were so easy. All those nice dinners you made, while we asked to use your computer, check our email. Like, what is it you Americans say? Stealing candy from a baby."

Della wavered a little, taking it all in. So they were right—she had been part of the leak that nearly allowed the formula to be stolen. It was all happening, all under her nose, and she never had a clue.

"We had to get into your home, into your computer, and have the time to do it—being good friends was the easiest way, and asking for your help on the wedding, which you were so eager to give, was the perfect distraction. It's almost a little sad," Chloe said with a mean-hearted chuckle.

Della stared at her, disbelieving, and suddenly very angry. "The only thing sad here is *you*," she said softly to Chloe. "Selling out your country, your friends, for *him*? And you call me desperate? You know you were just part of his plan, and that he'll probably do to you what he does to everyone he works with. Why do you think you'd be different?"

This time Chloe raised her hand, and Della flinched, but Justin—or rather, Cedric—stopped her from following through with the strike.

"Not yet, love. Later, we can have all the fun we want with her."

He turned to Nick, who looked like he wanted to kill Derian on the spot.

"You have some work to do, Gabe. Oh sorry—Nick. We need the rest of the formula. You're going to get it for us."

"Fat chance."

Cedric laughed. "Well, you see, now we have some insurance. At first, your presence was quite a problem, but then…a bonus. Especially since you and Della clearly care for each other. You would do anything you need to in order to save her, yes? Maybe I will give you that chance."

"You will not lay one hand on her, or—"

Cedric stepped up close to Nick. "Oh, I will do *much* more than that, I promise you, if you don't get me what I want."

Nick shook his head. "It's been moved to a secure facility. I might be able to get in, but it's going to take time, and I'll only do it if you let her go."

"You are not in any position to make the terms," Cedric said, moving back toward Della. "She is nothing to me, I could kill her now, and you, but I figured I would give you a chance."

Terrified, Della met Nick's eyes, but his expression was cool, inscrutable.

"Don't be scared, sweetheart. They're desperate because the people who wanted that formula are on their backs. They are very likely dead if they can't deliver. Who is it that you're so afraid of, Derian? What do you think they're going to do to *your* pretty new wife when they find you?"

Della saw Chloe flinch, and Derian took a few more steps toward Nick, clearly angry. As he lifted the gun in Nick's direction, she spoke quickly.

"But why did you follow me, wreck my home?"

Cedric stopped, as Chloe spoke.

"We hoped that would drive you to us, that you would come stay with us, and we would deliver you to our…partners. That's what we're going to do anyway, if your boyfriend here can't get us what we want."

"But why? I'm of no value."

Derian shrugged. "They don't know that, and short of handing them the formula, all we have to do is convince them you know more than you do. While they take their time torturing it out of you, we'd have time to disappear. Never go back empty-handed, and always have a plan B," he said with a cruel smile.

"Unless he—ol' Nick, there—can get the rest of the formula to us by tomorrow night, no later. Then perhaps we will let you live."

Della's heart sank, her shoulders drooping. "I doubt that very much. Don't do anything they tell you," she pleaded, speaking to Nick. "That's my choice. Whatever happens here, it's not your fault."

She needed him to know that, because of what happened with Janet. She saw the agony on his face.

"I'll do whatever it takes," he said, sliding his gaze to Derian. "I can find it. I'll get it, but only if you let her go. I don't care what you do to me, but if you don't let her go now, we all lose. You get nothing."

"Nick, no," Della gasped.

"You're all that matters to me, Della—period."

Her heart caught in her chest, and then she saw it…a small red light reflected off of Cedric's forehead.

Then another, on the man holding Nick by the car.

It was surreal as the bullet whizzed by her, and Pieter crumpled to the pavement. In the next second, Cedric was hit, and he also dropped to the ground.

Nick slumped next to Pieter just as something sharp hit Della on the back of her head, and her knees gave out, too.

NICK SAW DELLA fall and his heart gave way, the pain in his shoulder nothing compared to the loss he felt when he saw her crumple to the ground.

All hell broke loose around them, guys coming in from the edges, appearing out of the darkness like ghosts, and he had no idea whose men they were—from his government, or Cedric's team, or both—as he crawled over to where Della lay on the ground.

She moaned when he touched her head. She wasn't shot, but hurt. His hand came away from her head covered in blood.

Someone grabbed him and reflexively, Nick fought back, rolling to shield Della's prone form as he did so.

He looked up into Derian's face, ragged and clenched in pain as he gripped his chest, the shirt of his tux covered in blood.

Derian muttered something vile and raised his gun toward them.

Nick pushed off and launched himself at the man's legs, hitting him hard as the shot went off. Derian went down again, and Nick crawled up over him, grabbing the arm that held the gun. He fought, and Nick struggled, aware of voices around him, but focused on Derian. The guy was still strong as a bull, even when shot.

Nick thought about Della, his only concern that he

couldn't let her fall into this man's hands. He brought his hand down hard, and the gun went flying.

Picking him up by the shirt, he shook the criminal. "I'll stop you no matter what it takes. I promise you that," he growled.

"That won't be necessary, Gabe…why don't you back off. You're bleeding all over our terrorist."

The familiar voice cut through the fog of his anger, and he looked slowly up to find Bart—and five other agents in combat clothing—standing around them, weapons drawn.

"What are you doing here?" he asked them vaguely, his head spinning.

"Saving your sorry butt," Bart said with a sharp grin. "C'mon, get up."

Nick felt woozy, and reached out for the hand his friend and boss offered, but when he stood his knees gave out.

Someone barked for EMTs, and Nick shook his head, trying to focus. It didn't work.

"Della? Where's Della?"

"She's fine. We got her. We got all of them," Bart said, which was the last thing Nick heard before everything went dark.

DELLA WOKE UP in a dimly lit room, alone, and bolted upward, until a very sharp pain in her head had her falling back to the soft bed.

"Yeah, fast moves aren't advisable for a few days, anyway," someone said.

It was a strange voice, and she opened her eyes, refocusing on the man who stood beside her bed. She didn't know him.

"Who are you? Why am I—"

Then she remembered—the wedding, the confrontation and the sound of shots fired. Nick had been shot, and she…

"What happened? Where's Nick?"

The man narrowed his eyes on her, nodding.

"You must mean Agent Ross. He's in surgery, but he'll be fine. Just needed to repair some of the damage to his shoulder."

Nick was in surgery? Hot tears burned behind her eyes, and she was unable to control sobs that seemed to take her over.

"Hey, he's going to be fine—you, too. This is just the shock working its way out, don't worry. We've all been there."

Della tried to get hold of herself, but she didn't seem to have her normal presence of mind to do so.

"You're with DHS, too?" she asked.

He nodded. "Agent Bart Lowe. I wanted to be here when you woke up, so I could ask you a few questions, and remind you of your…responsibilities," he said with a quick smirk. "But we'll have to talk more at length, later, when you feel up to it."

Della closed her eyes again, her head pounding and her heart hurting as she worried about Nick. That's right, she remembered him telling her no one knew their real names on his team—so that if someone was compromised, they couldn't give away the others.

"I guess I just blew the whole real-name thing," she said stupidly.

"It's okay, I knew his name, I just never let him know I knew. All part of being the boss."

She smiled a little, but that hurt, too.

"What happened exactly?"

"You were hit really hard. Serious concussion, a laceration and some swelling. You'll be okay, but they need you here under observation for a few days."

She shifted her head slightly, but even that seemed to encourage the pain.

"I need to ask you a few questions, and remind you also not to say anything to anyone about what happened over the last few weeks, okay? No one—not the police, or anyone other than me. Your clearance was raised to cover your knowledge of this event, and the people involved, so you are bound by that—do you understand?"

"I understand," she murmured, trying to fight falling back asleep.

"Just a few questions, then," he said.

Della answered his questions the best she could, until a nurse came in and hustled the agent out the door.

"These guys, they never know when to quit. You get some rest," she said to Della, kindly fixing her blankets. "Things will be much better tomorrow."

Della wondered about Nick, and if she would ever see him again as her mind and body started to sink back into sleep. She hoped so, because she still didn't know his last name. As she drifted into oblivion, she feared that maybe she never would.

As IT TURNED OUT, the nurse was right. And wrong.

The next time Della opened her eyes in the hospital, she felt much better—and then much worse. Physically, she was out of the woods, but emotionally…when she asked about Nick again, she was only told that he'd been released, and that was all they knew. The kind nurse who had hustled the other agent out of her room told her that Nick had come by, had come to see her, but Della hadn't been awake.

She supposed that was his goodbye. The only one she was going to get, she realized a few weeks later, as she had not heard from him again in all that time.

So often she was tempted to find out, to talk to Bart, to whomever could tell her anything about him, but she knew they wouldn't.

Was he back in D.C.? Off to a new assignment? Was that it? Just…gone?

She refused to let the hurt take hold. She was alive—they both were—and that was a miracle in itself. Maybe he hadn't been free to come visit her, or able. But even if he never came back, maybe that was for the best. She worked hard on convincing herself that that was true as she sorted out her life.

But no matter how she tried to go back to normal, nothing was the same. Two weeks before the start of the new semester, even her workplace didn't feel right anymore. Every time she passed Chloe's desk, all she could think about was how gullible she'd been—on so many fronts. She'd erased her online dating profile—as if she wanted to date anyone—and couldn't believe how stupid she felt for…all of it.

And yet…she also wouldn't trade it for anything.

She wouldn't trade a single moment with Nick, even the bad ones, and she couldn't help but be glad for how the whole thing had opened her eyes, even while breaking her heart and nearly taking her life.

Her life had been so protected, so narrow…for all of her education and travels, she really had no sense of the world at all. She'd quit the ivory tower, she thought. She needed to put herself out there, and see what happened.

As it turned out, the head of her department wouldn't allow her to resign, but he did offer her a year's sabbatical. She took it without question. She wasn't sure what she wanted to do—she would go to Italy, explore her options and keep her guest lecture commitment, and then see what she wanted to do.

It was reckless, leaving her teaching responsibilities behind, but all she knew was that she had to go. If she had died that evening, it would have been the only time she had really lived, those weeks with Nick.

She couldn't go back to her cloistered existence again. The glass she'd lived under her entire life had been shattered by this experience, and in some ways, she was glad.

Maybe she would teach math to kids who needed good teachers, or perhaps she'd find new research of her own to do, or write a book. Maybe she'd join the CIA, she thought with a grin…then shook her head. No thanks. She wasn't *that* adventurous.

Italy first, she thought resolutely as she closed her suitcases and left her home, unsure when she would be back. A cab took her to the airport, and soon she was boarded, settling in to start her adventure.

Alone, but that was okay, as well.

She took out a book and a headset, intent on practicing her Italian on the flight.

Just as she was getting comfortable, someone stood at her side, a khaki-clad, masculine thigh bumping her arm, causing her to nearly drop her book.

"Sorry, but I think I have the window," a familiar voice said.

Della's breath caught, and she was almost afraid to look up. Then she did, and her eyes met a set of café au lait irises, or maybe they were more of a lionish gold… she never had really settled on that, though she also knew they tended to change according to his mood. Sometimes, in the dark, when they were alone, she could swear they turned the color of melted chocolate.

"Um, you might have to stand up so I can get in there, if that's okay?"

Della blinked. It *was* Nick…looking at her as if they had never met before. Talking to her like a stranger.

Perplexed, she nodded as she noted the impatience of the people standing behind him, and slipped out of her seat long enough for him to slide in and take the one next to her. She saw then that under the sport jacket he wore, his left arm was still in a light sling.

"Thanks," he said in relief, turning to her with a smile. "I'm Nick. Nicholas A. Lassiter."

Della's heart leaped in her chest and she looked at the hand he held out, worried that she might be completely imagining this, or worse, that she was suffering some kind of mental breakdown, and only imagined this was Nick sitting here with her.

"Della," she managed, lifting her hand to his. "Della Clark."

"Nice to meet you, Della."

Nick Lassiter, she thought. Lassiter. His real name. She couldn't play anymore. No more games.

"What are you doing here? Why now? I assumed…"

His expression changed, becoming intense, apprehensive, and…nervous? Nick, nervous?

"I'm sorry. The last few weeks were…tough. I saw you in the hospital, unconscious, and I knew that you had almost been killed because of me…because I put you in that path of danger. I knew I had to get as far away from you as I could, to stay away…but I couldn't."

She swallowed, her fingers tightening into fists around the edge of the armrests as the door on the plane closed. No escape now. She couldn't get up, couldn't get out. For better or worse, she was trapped with Nick on a plane, again, for the next seven hours.

NICK WASN'T SURE what to do, even though he had it all planned out in his mind. When he'd called the university, and found out that Della was on sabbatical, that she was heading to Italy, he'd had to pull the few strings he had left with Bart to find out which flight, and when.

"That's why I'm here. Because I realized, finally, that I couldn't stay away," he said baldly, watching her expression, her body so tensely held in the seat.

He wanted to touch her, to stroke away the tension, but not yet.

"You stayed away for weeks. I figured you had… moved on."

He nodded. "I tried. I convinced myself it would be best, for both of us. I didn't believe that I could make up for the lies, or for what happened. And even if you could forgive me, I couldn't forgive myself for not seeing Derian, so many times, right in front of me. I still don't know how I missed it. Missed him. So close to you," he said, pausing as he searched for the words.

"He didn't look anything like the photos," she agreed blankly. "He didn't even have an accent, and he had Chloe covering for him, inventing his backstory about their college romance. There was no way to know. How did you figure it out? How did you end up out at the car with them that night?"

"When we were in the church the night before, at the rehearsal, there was something about the best man that kept bugging me, something familiar. I realized I'd seen the tattoo on his arm in the files that came with the information on Derian. They both had it—he was Cedric's brother, Pieter. It didn't hit me until I was at the reception and by the time I put it all together, it was too late."

"But not before you had a chance to let Bart know?"

"I left my phone on the table with a coded message, and just hoped to hell he got it—he didn't, but he'd been tracking me since he set me loose. Good thing, as it turned out, or we probably wouldn't be sitting here."

She remembered the gunshots, the confusing chaos around her as she had fallen to the pavement, in too much pain to move.

"I saw you get shot. I saw the blood on your shirt. That was the last thing I remembered," she said thinly, her fingers still holding on to the armrests for dear life as they made their ascent. He didn't know if she was afraid of the takeoff, as she had once mentioned to him, or if she was afraid of him.

The thought shook him.

"But surely someone told you I was okay?" he asked, frowning.

"Bart did, and the nurse told me that…you had come to see me and then left. I hoped maybe when I was in D.C., being debriefed, you would be there. But you weren't."

"My debriefing was considerably more in-depth, it took a while, because I quit. I had to report on what happened with you, and Derian, but also close every case I had been involved in. It turns out there's a lot more paperwork and steps to go through getting out of the DHS than there is getting in," he said with a light laugh, turning to look out the window.

She was stunned. "What? You quit your job? Why?"

"It wasn't right anymore. Too much happened after this…after I met you. Being with you made me come out of the dark place I'd buried myself in for all that time. Made me want to reconnect with life. With my family. I had to get my head straight, so I went out to Denver, saw my brother and his wife and kids, and tried to decide what was the right thing to do."

"And that helped?"

"Seeing them, it clarified everything. I knew that all that matters, really, is being with the people you love. My work was important, sure, but I'm ready to move on to something new."

She looked wary, still, and unsure. That stung his heart, but Nick knew he'd earned her lack of trust. He took a deep breath.

"I love you, Della. I know that might sound crazy, and I'm not trying to scare you, or pressure you, but even if you can't forgive me, or never want to see me again, I needed to tell you. And…" he said, taking a chance to take her icy fingers from the armrest and wrap them in his own. "And to thank you. For giving me my life back."

"Nick, I—"

He interrupted, needing to get it all out before she shot him down.

"I guess what I was hoping, that eventually, maybe, after some time, maybe you might want to share that life with me. If you can ever forgive the lies, and that you were almost killed, because of me."

She swallowed hard, but didn't take her hand away. In fact, she leaned in, meeting his gaze.

"I didn't almost get killed because of you—I ended up in that situation because of *me*. Derian was right about one thing—I was gullible, and so...desperate," she said on a note of self-disgust, "to have friends, to be connected, that I never questioned anything about them or the situation. I never gave myself enough credit. There were small signs along the way, strange things that happened, but I ignored them, and my instincts. Except when it came to you. I couldn't ignore what I felt for you," she said softly. "Even when it hurt. Even now. I needed my eyes opened, I guess."

He held his breath and asked, "What do you feel? For me?"

She paused for several beats as the plane leveled out at altitude.

"I knew I loved you at the cabin... I knew it because of how terrible I felt when I thought it was all fake, all a ploy, when I found the tracker, and then, even after that, how I couldn't stop wanting you, even knowing you didn't feel the same."

He squeezed her hand in his. "But I did, and I do. I just didn't know how to deal with it. Can you believe me, Della? And if you can't, can you give me the time to prove it to you? I want to spend every day showing you how much I love you, if you'll let me."

Her features softened and she looked at him so tenderly Nick's chest tightened.

"You don't have to prove anything, Nick. Maybe we can just...be together. Start over. I can hardly believe you're here. That you're real. That any of this is real."

She let go of the other armrest to put her palm on

his cheek, and he felt like he could breathe for the first time in weeks. Turning his face into her hand, he kissed her soft skin, and felt everything in his life finally fall into place.

"This is very real, Della. Though now I'm wishing I had tried to meet you in Italy, when you landed... seven hours of being so close and not being able to touch you—really touch you—is going to drive me crazy," he said self-deprecatingly.

To prove his point, he slid his hand into her hair and took her lips in a kiss that exploded with so much heat they were both breathing more heavily when they parted.

"I'm sure we can find a way to pass the time," she said, her cheeks flushed, eyes bright. Reaching down into her bag, she pulled out her deck of cards.

Nick laughed, a full, happy laugh that he hadn't remembered doing since...well, a very long time ago. Della grinned.

"Maybe when we land," he said, leaning close, his hand sliding up her thigh, "we can have that game of strip poker we never got to before."

"Oh, most definitely."

Their laughter quieted, and he reached over, pulling her to him again, her face close to his. "I will never lie to you again, Della, ever. I want you to know that. No matter what. I'll never let anything hurt you."

When her eyes met his, they were full with unshed tears.

"We can't promise that we'll never be hurt. I know that now, and it's okay. I love you, Nick Lassiter." She beamed, taking another kiss. "Nice name, by the way. Very sexy. But what is the A for?"

He winced. "August."

She pulled back. "Nicholas August Lassiter? Is that the month you were born in?"

"No, I'm named after my grandfather Auggie."

She smiled. "I like it. And I like knowing it. I want to know everything about you."

"All you have to do is ask. I'm all yours, Della, for as long as you want me."

She set the cards aside, snuggling down into his shoulder as they floated over the clouds, into their future.

"That's going to be pretty much forever, then."

"Forever sounds perfect to me," he agreed, kissing the top of her head and holding her close, planning never to let her go again.

* * * * *

#855 ROLLING LIKE THUNDER
Thunder Mountain Brotherhood
by Vicki Lewis Thompson

Chelsea Trask might just be able to save the financially troubled ranch Finn O'Roarke once called home—if the scorching chemistry between her and the sexy brewmaster leaves them any time to work at all!

#856 THE MIGHTY QUINNS: DEVIN
The Mighty Quinns
by Kate Hoffmann

When Elodie Winchester returns to her hometown, Sheriff Devin Cassidy wants to reignite the passion between them, even if it costs him everything he's worked for...and exposes a shocking family secret.

#857 SEX, LIES AND DESIGNER SHOES
by Kimberly Van Meter

Rian Dalton likes to keep his business separate from pleasure. Until he meets client CoCo Abelli, an heiress with a reckless streak. Now Rian can't keep his hands to himself!

#858 A COWBOY RETURNS
Wild Western Heat
by Kelli Ireland

He's back. Eli Covington was Regan Matthews's first love—but not the man she married. Working together to save his New Mexico ranch brings up old feelings that are far too tempting to resist.

REQUEST YOUR FREE BOOKS!
2 FREE NOVELS PLUS 2 FREE GIFTS!

red-hot reads!

SPECIAL EXCERPT FROM

Police Chief Devin Cassidy can't resist reigniting the passion between him and Elodie Winchester, even if it costs him everything—and exposes a shocking connection to the Quinn family.

Here's a sneak preview of
THE MIGHTY QUINNS: DEVIN,
the latest steamy installment in
Kate Hoffmann's
beloved miniseries
THE MIGHTY QUINNS.

Elodie hurried downstairs and threw open the front door. She stepped out into the storm, running across the lawn. When she reached the police cruiser, she stopped. "What are you doing out here?" she shouted above the wind.

Dev slowly got out of the car, his hand braced along the top of the door. "I couldn't sleep."

"I couldn't, either," she shouted.

It was all he needed. He stepped toward her and before she knew it, she was in his arms, his hands smoothing over the rain-soaked fabric of her dress. His lips covered hers in a desperate, deeply powerful kiss. He molded her mouth to his, still searching for something even more intimate.

The fabric of her dress clung to her naked skin, a feeble barrier to his touch. Elodie fought the urge to reach for the hem of her dress and pull it over her head. They were on a public street, with houses all around.

HBEXP0715

"Come with me," she murmured. She laced her fingers through his and pulled him toward the house.

Once they reached the protection of the veranda, he grabbed her waist again, pulling her into another kiss. Dev smoothed his hand up her torso until he found her breast and he cupped it, his thumb teasing at her taut nipple.

Elodie reached for the hem of his shirt, but it was tucked underneath his leather utility belt. "Take this off," she murmured, frantically searching for the buckle.

He carefully unclipped his gun and set it on a nearby table. A moment later, his utility belt dropped to the ground, followed by his badge and, finally, his shirt. Her palms skimmed over hard muscle and smooth skin. His shoulders, once slight, were now broad, his torso a perfect V.

Dev reached for the hem of her dress and bunched it in his fists, pulling it higher and higher until it was twisted around her waist. He gently pushed her back against the door and she moaned as his fingertips skimmed the soft skin of her inner thigh.

Wild sensations raced through her body and she trembled as she anticipated what would come next...

Don't miss
THE MIGHTY QUINNS: DEVIN by Kate Hoffmann,
available August 2015 wherever
Harlequin® Blaze® books and ebooks are sold.

www.Harlequin.com

Love the Harlequin book
you just read?

Your opinion matters.

Review this book on your favorite
book site, review site, blog or your own
social media properties and share
your opinion with other readers!

Be sure to connect with us at:
Harlequin.com/Newsletters
Facebook.com/HarlequinBooks
Twitter.com/HarlequinBooks

THE WORLD IS BETTER WITH

Romance

Harlequin has everything from contemporary, passionate and heartwarming to suspenseful and inspirational stories.

Whatever your mood, we have a romance just for you!

Connect with us to find your next great read, special offers and more.

f /HarlequinBooks

🐦 @HarlequinBooks

www.HarlequinBlog.com

www.Harlequin.com/Newsletters

◆ HARLEQUIN®

A *Romance* FOR EVERY MOOD™

www.Harlequin.com